RIVER PILOT

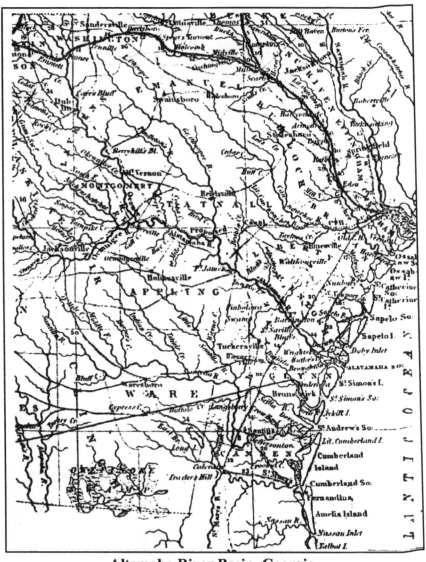

Altamaha River Basin, Georgia

RIVER PILOT

by

William V. Reynolds

Double Eagle Enterprises, Inc.
Murphy. NC

Author's Note

Although this book uses accounts given to the author about real people, it is a work of fiction. With the exception of the names of the immediate Reynolds and Hester families, all names are fictitious and should in no way be construed to be actual persons, living or dead.

Library of Congress Cataloging-in-Publication Data

ISBN:0-9700320-0-5

Printed in the United States of America

Pathway Press   Cleveland, TN

Contents

Dedication

This book is affectionately dedicated to the women in my life:

My wife:　　　　Joyce

My Daughters:　Pam & Eva

And to the memory of:

My mother:　　　Lois

My grandmother: Eva

Chapter 1
Doctor Town

"**G**us!

"Gus! I can't see a damn thing in this fog."

Felix King looked around at the fog that blanketed the Altamaha River in the early dawn of the spring morning. The world was awakening from its nocturnal sleep and the cool morning air sent a chill through Felix's bones that caused him to shiver in the quiet morning air.

Gus called from the other end of the raft, "We'll have to get movin' if we expect to make Doctor Town today."

The raft had been tied up over night because of the darkness and the ensuing fog that usually accompanied it. Rafting was sometimes done at night, but only by moonlight when visibility was good.

There was also the risk of meeting a steamboat on the Altamaha in the year 1908. The river served as a highway for commerce despite the fact that the railroads had come to South Georgia and taken a great deal of the freighting business from its waterways.

Gus stoked the fire that served as their source of heat and cooking. He added fresh kindling and more fuel to raise a blaze from the embers. A raised mound of earth on the raft served as a cradle for the fire to prevent water from dousing the flames.

Soon the smell of cooking came from the fire area. George and Felix joined Gus at the fire for a breakfast of bacon and eggs.

The raftsmen tidied up their breakfast leavings, dropping scraps of food into the river for the fish and washing their tin pans in the river water. Gus doused the fire since they would be delivering the raft today and would have no further need of it on this trip.

Ropes were loosed and sweeps were used to propel the raft into the channel. By now the fog was lifting and visibility was much better.

Guiding a timber raft is fairly simple as long as you have good water. The major problem is usually turning bends of the river, especially when the channel narrows and the waters become swift. Most of the treacherous waters were behind so the job was easy from here to Doctor Town.

The raftsmen didn't talk much except occasionally to banter each other good-naturedly. Mostly the pace was rather lazy and didn't require much exchange among crew members.

Gus kept an eye peeled for stray logs and snags that might lie just below the surface of the water. These snags could present a problem if they were anchored enough to cause the raft to rotate off course. An occasional pull of the sweeps was necessary to avoid a snag or correct the course of the raft when a snag caused it to veer off course.

A raft moves with the current of the river so you just have to be patient. This isn't work for those who would hurry.

There's plenty to watch as you float lazily along. Fish were jumping, sometimes in arches, sometimes almost straight up. Gus spied two otters chasing each other and competing for the catch of the nearest fish. Lazy old turtles lay on exposed logs sunning themselves. As the raft approached, they would slide off their perch and plunge into the water with a resounding plop. Water snakes could sometimes be seen, either swimming or sunning themselves on logs. George called attention to a mama moccasin lying in the sun with her brood wrapped over her. On shore, one might see a deer or even a black bear. There were a few alligators, but they were rarely visible.

The land was anything from a high bluff to a flooded swamp. The Altamaha river tends to have more bluff on the south side and more flat swamp on the north. Huge trees stood in abundance in the swamp and even the bluffs had trees, some of which were hanging precariously, waiting to plunge to the river below.

Finally, the raftsmen's persistence paid off. Doctor Town and the sawmill came into view. But seeing a place and being there are two different things. It was another hour's work to bring the raft alongside for delivery.

"Yo, Frank. We've got another one for you," Gus shouted, as the raft made contact with logs lying alongside the riverbank.

"I'll be down in a bit, Gus."

As Frank came down to the raft, he extended a hand to Gus in greeting. "Have a good trip?" he asked.

"Not bad. Just the usual," Gus answered.

"How much you got this time?"

Gus looked toward the raft and pushed back his hat. "This is the last one this season. I'd guess about 30,000 board feet."

Frank picked up his scale rule and started to measure the diameter of each log at the small end. He recorded the diameter and corresponding length of each log on a pad. When these records were complete, he moved off the raft and began to record a column of figures beside each log measurement, consulting the rule once in awhile since he had most of them memorized as a result of working with timber for so long.

"Man, you sure have an eye for this stuff," Frank announced. "I make it 29,600 board feet."

"I reckon that's close enough," Gus replied.

Frank turned and started up the river bank. "Come on up to the office and we'll get your money."

Gus, George, and Felix followed Frank up the river bank to the sawmill office, a small cramped space barely large enough to accommodate two people. Frank went inside and opened a box to retrieve some forms.

"Bank draft okay, Gus?" Frank asked.

"I guess so. Old man Youmans don't mind much as long as he gets his money, and I'd just as soon not carry cash. Too many crazies around who'll knock you in the head for it."

Frank filled out the bank draft, signed it, and handed it to Gus. "Have a safe trip home. You ridin' the train or walkin'?"

Gus pocketed the draft and buttoned his pocket. "We thought we'd splurge and ride the train since this's our last trip this spring. Got to get back to the farm and finish the spring plowin', you know."

"So long. See you next trip," Frank said, as the raftsmen left the sawmill on their trek to the railroad.

Doctor Town lay on the Altamaha River about five miles north of the railroad in Jesup, Georgia. It was basically a company sawmill town consisting of shanties put together with boards cut from the timber processed at the local sawmill. The housing was poor and so were the people who scratched out a living there. The dirt streets were mudholes during rainy weather and the town's proximity to the swamps made it an ideal breeding hole for mosquitoes when the weather was warm.

A railroad spur ran from Jesup to the mill to aid in the shipment of lumber from the sawmill, but there was no regular run between Doctor Town and Jesup. Gus decided to walk to Jesup, or catch a ride on someone's wagon. Besides, they really didn't have the money to squander on a fare to Jesup.

The company commissary served as the only source of food and supplies at the sawmill, but you could also get a drink there. Gus, George and Felix decided they needed some refreshments before beginning their hike to Jesup.

Felix was the first to the counter. "You got anything that'll grow hair on a man's chest?"

"We've got some of the best stuff made around this county," the proprietor boasted.

Glasses were set up and filled and everybody savored his drink.

"Anything else for you gents?" the proprietor inquired.

Gus finished his drink, set his glass on the counter, and wiped his mouth with his bandanna. "Guess not. You wouldn't know if anybody's headin' for Jesup would you? We could sure use a ride."

"Ain't nobody I know goin' that way this late in the day."

"Well, thanks anyway. Let's go, boys."

The raftsmen had plodded along for perhaps half a mile when they heard a wagon approaching from behind. They stepped out of the road to let the wagon pass. As the driver came alongside he pulled back on the reins and said, "Whoa."

"You fellers need a ride?"

"We sure could use one. I don't fancy a five mile walk to Jesup," Felix chimed.

"Hop on. I'll be goin' most of the way," the driver offered. "You fellers musta brought in a raft."

The raftsmen seated themselves on the lumber that covered the floor of the wagon. The driver spoke to his team, "Giddy up." The team began to move down the road at a steady gait.

Gus answered, "Yeah, we just landed her about noon."

Felix stretched himself out on the boards and covered his face with his hat and was presently asleep. Soon George decided to join him.

The wagon moved at a good pace and all in all the ride wasn't too bad except for the eternal bumping along the rutted road. Occasionally, other wagons would meet them and it was necessary for one or the other to pull off the narrow road in order for the other to pass.

The afternoon was well spent and the sun wasn't more than an hour high when the driver pulled his team to a halt and said, "This is as far as I go."

"Thanks for the ride," the raftsmen said, almost in unison as they dismounted.

The sun was setting as the raftsmen approached the railroad station. Gus went to the ticket window to purchase the tickets.

"We'll need three tickets for Baxley. What time does the train leave?"

The agent retrieved three tickets, reached for a stamp, stamped the tickets and said, "That'll be three dollars. Train leaves at midnight."

"Might as well get somethin' to eat while we wait," Gus suggested.

Felix grinned, raised his drooping eyelid, and said, "Just so it ain't your cookin'. I'm tired of eatin' it."

Gus didn't show any reaction, but said, "That's okay. You can cook next trip."

A small café near the railroad station offered them a meal of meat, potatoes, and vegetables. Everybody ate heartily and enjoyed several cups of coffee.

George was the youngest of the trio, in his late teens with a shock of unruly red hair, and had a healthy interest in the opposite sex. The young lady who waited on them naturally caught his attention.

"What you doin' after work?" he inquired.

"Most likely I'll be goin' home."

"How about me walkin' you home?"

"I don't know you. Why'd I let you do that?"

"So's we can get acquainted."

"I don't know."

"If you don't know, who does?"

"I'll have to think about it."

After the meal, the threesome sat outside the café on the loafers' bench and talked and listened to the sounds of the night. Felix took out his pipe, packed it full of tobacco, and lit up.

"Gus, how old are you anyway?" Felix inquired.

Gus looked at him and said, "Why, you takin' a census?"

"Nope. Just wondered why a feller your age ain't married with a passel of young'uns."

"Too busy workin' and helpin' out Ma and Pa, I reckon."

"Ain't you sweet on none of them gals at Spring Branch?"

"I've danced with a few of 'em, but nothin' serious. Besides it takes a lot of money to get married and have a family. I happen to be short on that right now."

"Shaw, it ain't that bad. Why me and my missus started out with practically nothin'. Yore Pa's got all that land and timber, there's bound to be a place for you and a family there somewheres."

"I might tie the knot sometime, if I find the right girl."

The café door opened and the waitress who had served their

meal stepped out wrapped in her shawl. George sprang up from the loafers' bench and intercepted her in mid-stride.

"Hey, wait a minute. What about me walkin' you home?"

She paused and looked at him shyly. "I reckon. What's your name, anyhow?"

"George, George Hester," he said, with a short breath.

"Mind you, I've got to go straight home, and there won't be no lolly-gaggin' around. My Pa won't allow it. 'Sides, he ain't too fond of strangers."

"I won't be no stranger when we get there, you can introduce me proper then."

"I'll be back in awhile," George said, as he turned to follow her down the boardwalk.

Gus called after him, "Don't be long, that train leaves at midnight with or without you."

Felix took another draw on his pipe and sighed, "Aw, them was the days. Oh, to be young again."

"I wouldn't know," Gus remarked.

Gus and Felix made their way back to the depot and decided to catch a nap since the train wasn't due for a couple of hours. They each settled on a bench and lay back covering their eyes with their hats.

Gus slept soundly for perhaps two hours. A slight movement somewhere in the depot awakened him and he sat up, rubbing the sleep from his eyes. Felix lay snoring contentedly.

Gus checked the clock on the wall. It was 12:15 A. M. Either he'd slept through the train, or it was late. He decided to check with the agent.

"What happened to the midnighter?"

"Oh, it's runnin' late. That's normal when there's lots of switchin' to do."

"Is that any way to run a railroad?" Gus joked.

The agent ignored him and continued reading the forms in his hand.

Suddenly, it dawned on Gus that George wasn't back yet. Where is that boy? he thought.

In the distance a train whistle sounded for the station. Felix jumped like he'd been shot, fell off the bench he'd been sleeping on, and landed on his butt on the floor.

"Felix!" Gus called. "Here's our train. I don't know where George is. I guess he got to gazin' into that gal's eyes and forgot to check the time."

Felix got up, dusting the seat of his breeches, and said, "What the heck, he's got his ticket. Let him catch the next train."

"I guess we don't have a choice. I have to get back. I've got lots of work that needs to be done."

The steam locomotive huffed and puffed into the station and came to a stop accompanied by a screech of brakes. The conductor stepped down and placed a step for a couple of passengers. "We'll be here about five minutes, folks."

Gus and Felix boarded the passenger car and found a seat near the rear of the car. Gus sat back and pulled his hat down over his eyes.

"All abooardd!" the conductor called.

The train engine puffed a roll of smoke and the drive wheels slipped as the locomotive was engaged. The train started to move slowly forward.

Gus heard a voice yell, "Hey, wait for me!"

George caught the rail and swung himself aboard just as the train gained enough speed so that he wouldn't have been able to get on board. Out of breath, George stood on the car platform and breathed hard for a minute. Strolling inside he said, "I almost didn't make it."

"We thought you'd got lost in them brown eyes," Felix ribbed him.

George grinned, "She was a looker all right. We got to talkin' and I completely lost track. Had to run most all the way to catch the train."

"Uh huh," Felix grunted.

The train ride from Jesup to Baxley would take somewhere around an hour if it were non-stop, but this train served more than one purpose so stops were frequent. Odum and Surrency were regular stops, and sometimes other sidings like Wheaton required attention.

Felix had had a good nap at Jesup, so he wanted to talk. Gus suffered in silence as he and George bantered each other. Felix had a tale he just had to tell.

"George, did you know some of these new-fangled trains have outhouses on them?"

"You don't say! You're kiddin', right?"

"I'm serious as a heart attack."

"How do they work?"

Felix warmed up to his story and continued. "Well, you see these outhouses, they call'em 'privies', are right here on the train and you go in there and do your business right on the tracks."

"No!"

"Sure you do. This feller who'd never been on a train told the conductor to stop the train 'cause he had to go. The conductor says, 'Why don't you try our privy?'

"So this gent goes and does his thing and about the time he gets through a cinder flies up and hits his butt. When he comes out the conductor asks him how it was. He looks at the conductor sort of serious-like and says, 'It was okay, but I got to tell you, that autermatic tailwiper is gonna hurt somebody.'"

George rewarded Felix with a hearty laugh. Gus grinned and said, "Will you two pipe down and go to sleep?"

The train rumbled on through the night.

Chapter 2
The Farm

Baxley, Georgia, was little more than a frontier town in the early 1900s. The streets were unpaved, many of the buildings were clapboard, unsealed structures that barely kept the weather out, and sidewalks were simply the joining of the front porch of one establishment to that of another. It would be another twenty years before a paved road ran through the town.

Agriculture, including forestry, was the mainstay of the local economy. Several turpentine distilleries lay near the town and in the surrounding county of Appling. Family farms were common and cash crops consisted of cotton, tobacco, and corn. Forestry products included lumber, turpentine, and rosin.

County government was now located in Baxley, having been moved from Holmesville some distance to the southeast. This meant the court house, jail, and sheriff's office were now more centrally located in the newly reduced county of Appling. The new county was about a third of the former size, having been divided to form the new counties of Bacon and Jeff Davis. These were truly horse and buggy counties since most residents could now reach their county seats in one day by means of horse drawn vehicles.

The train carrying Gus, George, and Felix rolled into this sleepy little town early in the morning and ground to a stop at the local depot. The travelers exited the train and headed north along what served as a main street. Gus's family's farm lay about five miles north in the Spring Branch community. George and Felix would head northwest into Jeff Davis county. They said their farewells and went their separate ways.

Gus knew he was in for a hike, since it was highly unlikely

anyone would be out this early on the roads. Gus wound his way along a narrow road that would someday be the path of a modern highway called U.S.#1. It took him the better part of two hours to complete his journey. He was in no hurry, since he knew the family wouldn't be out and about for another hour.

Life on the farm revolved around the daylight hours. It was often said that farmers worked from sun to sun, meaning sunup to sundown. Farm work was exhausting so farmers tried to work mostly in the cool of the day and take a long noon hour.

Alonzo, Gus's father, was an early riser. He practiced this partly because of the weather and otherwise because he was simply a morning person--one who awakens and is ready to rise and be about his business.

There were chores to be done, so after building a fire in the stove in the kitchen, he would call the children and send them about the morning chores while he joined in himself. The milking had to be done; the pigs and cows fed; and the draft stock, horses and mules, fed and attended for the coming day of labor on the farm.

Meanwhile, Susie, Gus's mother, would prepare a country breakfast consisting of fresh eggs gathered from the hen house that morning; ham, bacon, or sausage from the smokehouse; grits ground from the family's own corn; and delicious cat-head biscuits served with a pitcher of milk from the family cow; and syrup made from the family's cane patch. Flour and coffee were the most common items purchased by the family. Otherwise, they produced almost all of their food on the farm.

Gus could smell the enticing aroma of Susie's warm breakfast as he approached the house in the early morning dawn. The sounds of the farm coming to life greeted his ears. The horses were whinnying in anticipation of their morning feed, the pigs were grunting and squealing as they fought over which one would claim a place at the trough, and the cows lowed as they came to the barn for their morning feed.

"Ya'll come and eat breakfast now," Susie called from the kitchen door.

From various points around the house, Alonzo and the children converged on the kitchen which was set apart from the house for fire safety. Gus walked up just in time to join the group as they entered the warm enclosure and seated themselves at the table.

"Pa! Gus is home," cried Tom, the youngest of the boys.

"So he is. How was the trip, boy?" Alonzo asked.

"Everything went pretty smooth, Pa. Had to retie some ropes a couple of times when the river got rough and started shaking us apart, but that's normal on parts of that river."

"It's sure good to have you home. Let's eat."

The family bowed their heads and Alonzo gave thanks. "Lord, we thank you for seein' Gus home safe and sound and we thank you for all your other blessin's. Give us strength from the food we are about to receive and we'll give you the honor. Amen."

Susie passed Gus the grits and said, "Eat up, boy. I know you haven't been eating good all the time you was gone."

Mothers were always mothers, Gus thought. It didn't matter how old you were, you were still a little kid to them.

He said, "Thanks, Ma. I was gettin' tired of my own cookin'."

Gus helped himself to a generous portion of the grits, two slices of bacon, slid a couple of eggs onto his grits and stirred them in. A large biscuit topped the plate and a steaming cup of coffee completed the feast.

Alonzo spoke between bites of food, concerning work that had to be done on the farm. "That back field needs plowin'. I reckon you'd better take Sam with you and see if the two of you can finish it today."

Gus finished chewing a mouthful of food, sipped some coffee and answered, "Okay, Pa. We ought to be able to do it in a day if old Doc don't go lame on us again."

Alonzo paused a moment and frowned. "I'd get rid of that ornery piece of horsemeat if I could find somebody that'd take him off my hands. He's been nothing but trouble ever since I bought him. I ought to shoot that shyster that sold him to me."

Gus took another sip of coffee, "I think you'll have to shoot the horse, Pa. Ain't nobody in his right mind gonna buy him."

After breakfast each of the children went about their daily routine. The younger ones still had a few days of school to attend so they left for Spring Branch School which was about a mile's distance from the family home. Alonzo believed that his children should learn to read and write and do their sums, so he seldom kept them at home during the six months school term.

Gus suddenly remembered that he still had the bank draft from the timber sale in his pocket. "Ma, if Uncle Homer comes by, would you give him this bank draft and tell him I'll be on the back forty if he needs to talk?"

"Sure, son. I'll tell him," Susie said, as she stowed the paper in a canister on the kitchen shelf. "I'll fix you and Sam a nice jug of water to take to the field and you can come to the house about noon for dinner."

Gus looked at Sam who was finishing his third, or was it his fourth glass of milk. "Sam, let's get goin' before that sun gets too hot."

Sam wiped his mouth on his sleeve and said, "Okay, I'm coming."

Gus and Sam went to the stable to hitch up for the day's plowing. Gus decided he would use the horse, Doc, so he took the bridle from the tack room and opened the lot gate to place it on the horse. Sam would use the mule, Jack.

Each animal was outfitted with a collar and a set of hames. The collar served as a cushion around the shoulders of the animal while the hames fit over the collar and provided rings to fasten trace chains. The trace chains were then fastened to a single-tree attached to the front of the plow. The plows were one-horse, plows designed to be pulled by one animal, turning plows.

As Gus and Sam came by the house on their way to the field, Susie came from the kitchen carrying a small stone jug and a small basket filled with leftover biscuits from breakfast. "Here's a jug of water and a snack in case you get hungry before noon," she said, handing them to Gus.

"Thanks, Ma," Gus said, as he handed the basket to Sam and cradled the jug under his arm. "We'll be back for dinner."

When Gus and Sam arrived in the field, they went to a tree and stashed their water in a hole in the ground shaded by the base of the tree, and hung the basket on a limb that had been cut off about six feet above the ground. This kept the water as cool as possible and prevented varmints from stealing their food.

Gus cut the first furrow and Sam followed him as they tilled the soil to prepare it for planting. It was necessary to stop frequently and let the animals cool from their work. This also gave the brothers an opportunity to rest and chat. They usually took refuge in the shade of a tree and sometimes took a swig of water and or ate some of the biscuits Susie had sent.

Gus and Sam toiled until their shadows began to shorten so that they could almost step on the head of their shadows. When you didn't have a watch this was a fairly accurate clock to tell when noon arrived.

The brothers unhitched the animals, leaving their plows in the field, and walked them to the stables. There they fed them their noon-day ration of corn and hay.

Susie called from the kitchen door, "Ya'll wash up. Dinner'll be ready in a few minutes."

A wash stand on the breezeway between the house and the kitchen held a bucket of water and a washpan. A cake of home-made lye soap served as a cleansing agent. You had to be careful though because the soap would take your skin off almost as easily as it did the dirt.

Sam finished washing his hands and flung the dirty water into the yard. Reaching for a towel, he pushed the pan to Gus who filled it from the bucket and began to scrub his hands.

"Ya'll be sure and get your hands clean. I don't want no grime left on my towels," Susie said, as she exited the kitchen.

By the time Gus and Sam seated themselves at the table, all the rest of the family were there, except the school children who carried their lunches. Alonzo gave thanks and the meal was under way.

The meal consisted of green beans, corn, sliced ham, and cornbread. Hearty fare for working folks.

"Gus, Homer ain't been by today. You don't reckon he's forgot about his money?" Susie asked.

Gus finished a mouthful of food. "It ain't likely. He'll need that money to settle his debts and buy supplies for spring plantin'. If he don't come by for it in the next day or two, I'll take it to him.

"Pa, me and Sam should finish that back forty this evenin'. When you figure we'll be ready to start plantin'?" Gus inquired.

"Well, I got the seed a couple of days ago, so I reckon we'll start tomorrow or maybe Monday."

"That's good. I was hoping to get to town a bit on Saturday."

"I think that can be arranged."

The meal continued in silence. Finally, Alonzo pushed back his plate, looked across the table at Susie and gave her his highest compliment, "Old woman, that potlicker was mighty good."

Susie's face betrayed a slight smile as she said, "Thank you."

After the meal, most of the family would "noon," rest a while, usually taking a nap. Gus usually found a spot on the breezeway or front porch and lay there with his hat over his eyes to shut out the light while he slept.

The sound of hoofs and the rattle of a buggy awakened Gus as Homer Youmans drove into the front yard. "Hello! Anybody home?" Homer called as he reined in his horse.

"It sure is hard for a feller to get any sleep around here," Gus grinned as he went through the front gate to meet Homer.

"Well, some of us have to work for a livin'," Homer returned. "You got something for me?"

"Yep. Ma's got it stashed in the kitchen somewhere. I give it to her this mornin'. Get down and rest yourself a spell."

"I'd like to, but I got to get to town before the bank closes. Got to meet them payments so I'll be able to plant crops this year."

"I'll get your money."

Gus went around the house to the kitchen and found his mother tidying up. "Uncle Homer's out front. Where'd you put that bank draft, Ma?"

Susie reached up and retrieved the draft from the canister, handed it to Gus and asked, "Did you invite Homer in?"

"Yes, ma'am, but he's in a hurry to get to town before the bank closes."

Gus returned to the front yard, handed Homer the draft, and laughed, "Don't spend it all in one place."

"Ain't no need to worry about that. As many people as I owe, I have to go down one side the street payin' and down the other apologizin'," Homer said, as he slapped the reins and drove off in a swirl of dust.

"Sam! We got to get movin'. That plowin' ain't gonna do itself," Gus called as he came around the house and headed for the barn.

Doc decided to cooperate for once and Gus and Sam completed the backfield before the sun set. Returning to the stable, they fed and watered the animals and got themselves ready for supper.

* * *

Saturday morning came and the planting was begun. Planting a crop required more work than simply breaking the ground.

First, you had to open the row. This was done either by using a plow commonly called a middle buster or by running two furrows with a turning plow. The last operation required twice as much work, but the first was more strain on the animals.

Next, fertilizer was distributed. Fertilizers usually consisted of compost from the feed lots of the animals. On rare occasions a farmer might purchase bat guano which had been shipped by train from various parts of the country or even South America.

Now the seed, which had been saved when possible from last year's crop, was bedded in the row. The total process required at least three trips over the field. The best part was that you could now wait until the seed had sprouted and grown before you began the battle with the grasses.

After dinner on Saturday, the family decided to take some

time off from the planting and do some things around the house. Gus took advantage of this time to make his trip to Baxley. A bath, shave, and change of clothes made him feel more presentable.

"Pa, is it okay if I take one of the horses?" Gus asked as he prepared to leave.

"I reckon. Don't tire him out though."

"He'll have all day tomorrow to rest."

Gus turned to his mother, "Is there anything I can bring you from town, Ma?"

"You might fetch us some coffee and a sack of flour, son."

Gus saddled a horse and rode off toward Baxley as the family waved. He returned the wave and nudged the horse with his knees to spur him to a faster pace.

Saturday night was bath night. Water was drawn from the well beside the breezeway and wash tubs were filled and placed in the sunlight in order to warm the water. If the weather was cold, the kitchen, which could be warmed with the stove, served as the bathroom.

Susie would inspect the work of the younger children, checking behind their ears and elbows to make sure these hadn't been missed. Then others in the household would take their turn in the bath.

Alonzo had worn a beard most of his life. He said he had shaved twice in his life, once in a horse trough with lye soap, and again with a dull razor. Afterward, he had decided it wasn't worth the effort. Consequently, Susie would give him a hair and beard trim on Saturday nights.

Gus was gone until well into the night. He came home quietly during the night, and although he wasn't drunk, if anyone had checked they probably would have smelled alcohol on his breath. He went to bed and slept soundly until morning.

* * *

Sunday was church day. Not every Sunday, but twice a month, a preacher came to Spring Branch School and delivered a sermon. There was talk of building a church building, but it had never amounted to more than talk. And who needed to spend all that money and labor when they already had a meeting place?

Susie checked the children one more time to see if everything was in place. The girls were as neat as they could be, except Susan who had managed to smudge her face somehow. The boys were a different story. Tom hated to dress up. He much preferred his everyday togs to the Sunday suit Susie usually dressed him in. "Tom stand up straight and pack your shirt tail in. You're slouching something awful," Susie admonished him.

"Aw, Ma. Do I have to wear these dumb ole clothes? I wanta play and you won't let me dirty these."

"Yes, sir! You're going to wear something nice to church. You can change after you get home."

Susie herded the children out to the wagon, "Get on up now, your Pa'll be along in a minute."

Alonzo came from the house wearing his Sunday suit and looking all spruced up. Susie admired him, and as he approached the wagon she gave him her ultimate compliment, "Old man, you look better with your beard trimmed."

"Thank you, ma'am," Alonzo replied with a grin.

Gus joined the family as they started for the church meeting. He sat in the back of the wagon with his feet dangling and joined the children in a song.

The crowd was beginning to gather at the school house and it seemed the school yard would soon fill with horses and wagons. People usually turned out for services unless the weather was unfavorable. They came in horse drawn conveyances of all sorts. They would walk, if they were near enough.

The men gathered around and talked farming. The ladies formed a group and caught up on the latest social news. The children chased each other around the building with subdued voices since their mothers had threatened them within an inch of their lives if they made too much noise. The older boys stood in a group and looked at the older girls, sometimes laughing and making a joke with one another. Most of the older girls would glance their way and then hold their heads up and walk away as if to say, "Who do you think you are, anyhow?"

Reverend Butler had arrived, so everybody began to drift into the school house, some more reluctant than others. The women and children seated themselves on one side and the men and older boys on the other. Gus found a seat at the rear near the door. When all were seated, Reverend Butler picked up a hymnal and said, "It's good to see everybody today. Pick up your hymn book and let's sing 100."

The congregation followed as best they could as they sang, "Praise God from Whom All Blessings Flow...."

Gus joined in the singing and seemed to enjoy it. The sermon was another thing. It was mostly hellfire and brimstone, and he really would have preferred to take a nap, except Reverend Butler was too loud. To tell the truth, Gus wasn't much on religion, probably because he had some guilt and conflicts in his life that weren't resolved.

When the service was over, Gus slipped outside to wait for the family near the wagon. Soon everyone was in place and on their way.

Sunday was a day of rest for everyone. Nobody did anything except the bare minimum of feeding the stock. Sunday dinner was a quiet affair, then Sunday afternoon was spent playing games if you were a child and perhaps reading if you were an adult.

Alonzo was an avid reader of the Bible. He had read it through a number of times and would complete some fifty readings in his lifetime. Sunday afternoons gave him an opportunity to concentrate on his reading.

Gus wasn't an avid reader so he found other pursuits to occupy his time. One of his favorites was to take a walk in the woods, find a good shade under a tree, and simply sit and think.

He sometimes wondered where his life was going. Here I am 26 years old, he thought, and it seems I don't have much to look forward to. I'd like to take off and do some traveling and see the world, but Ma and Pa need me, and I can't very well just pick up and leave them. Life seemed mighty dull at the moment.

* * *

Monday morning arrived bright and early. The planting had to be finished, so the whole family, except the children who were in school, pitched in to help. Even so, the planting took another two weeks with frequent interruptions for rain.

As soon as the planting was completed, Gus went to work in the family woods. Most family farms had timberland consisting of large numbers of slash and yellow pines, from which they extracted the gum for sale to be refined into spirits of turpentine and rosin.

These trees were referred to as "boxes" because of the unique way the gum was gathered. Using a tool call a "box axe," a cavity was carved at the root of the tree to collect the gum. The gum ran from the tree as a result of cuts through the wood called "streaks." A series of streaks up the tree formed what was commonly known as a "face." About once a week the workers cut a new streak with an instrument called a "hack." After about a month, the workers gathered the gum in a bucket using a ladle with a two to three foot handle called a "paddle" or sometimes a "dipper."

This work, along with the row crop work, occupied most of Gus's time for the summer. He did manage to put away a little money though, and life didn't always seem dull. It wouldn't be long before he could return to the river swamps and the life he really liked best.

Chapter 3
Family Reunion

Summer gave way to Fall in 1908, and the harvest season began on the farm. Cotton had to be picked and hauled to the local gin, corn was gathered into the crib, and hay cut and baled. The turpentine faces would be scraped and the last gum of the season gathered. Winter would soon be here and preparation had to be made for the months when it would not be possible to gather food from the fields. Foods had been canned in jars or dried and preserved for the coming months. As soon as the weather was cool enough, the family would invite the neighbors to a hog killing, and the butchered meat would be smoked and salted.

Gus was busy with all of these activities, but would soon be leaving for the logging camp and his winter work of cutting and rafting timber. He really looked forward to the change.

Work was a driving force for survival on the farm, but the farm family also enjoyed social events. The family reunion was one of the social events most anticipated by members of the family.

The Reynolds family was remotely related to several families in the area, and therefore received invitations to a number of family reunions. Alonzo really got into genealogies on several occasions and had been heard to say, "Heck, that bunch is all one another's Grandpas anyhow."

The Reynolds family usually attended the Hall family reunion in Jeff Davis County each September. It was a chance to catch up on the latest happenings from all over the area since families from most of the surrounding counties would be there.

These events were not exactly Gus's favorites. However, he

decided to attend this year's reunion since it would be his last chance to socialize before heading for the logging camps. He helped make preparation for the journey to the reunion. The trip would take a day and it would be necessary to stay over night for at least one night.

"Gus, did you get them quilts in the wagon? We'll need 'em if the weather turns off cold," Susie called from the front door of the house.

"Yes, ma'am," Gus replied.

Susie turned back to the house to double check other items. "Alonzo, did you put the sack of potatoes and side of bacon in the food box?"

Alonzo came around the house bearing a burden. "Got 'em right here, Susie," he said, placing the items on the wagon.

"I reckon that's everything," Susie said, as she closed the front door and walked to the wagon. "If we left anything, we'll just do without it."

The family mounted the wagon, Alonzo slapped the reins and the horses moved off at a steady pace with a long stride. The wagon could have been driven faster, but the roads were rough, and the animals had to be paced so that they didn't tire too quickly.

The family entertained themselves in a variety of ways as they traveled. Sometimes they would sing or someone would tell a tale of some kind. Occasionally, they would play a guessing game or simply engage in friendly banter.

Sam had been quiet for sometime, lost deep in thought it seemed. "Pa?"

Alonzo glanced back, "What is it, son?"

"Where'd our family come from? How'd we get our name?"

This was one of Alonzo's favorite topics, so he launched into it with vigor. "Well, son, the family name goes back a long way. It seems there were Reynoldses living in England as far back as the 1200s.

"The name means 'son of reynold' or 'son of reignald.' If you check the meaning of reynold the first part seems to mean 'ruler' and the last part means 'elder.' So I guess you could say we're 'sons of the rulin' elders' or maybe 'sons of the elder ruler.'

"As to how we come to be in this country, that's not quite clear. It seems that seven brothers from England landed in Charlestown, South Carolina, several generations ago and settled in North and South Carolina. I know our family moved to Georgia from North Carolina, so I expect we're descended from one of those brothers.

"It might interest you to know that, according to family tradition, you have the blood of the Cherokee Indian running through your veins. You see, they say my Grandma was bought from a Cherokee Chief for a horse."

"Alonzo, don't go tellin' these young'uns wild tales," Susie interrupted.

"As near as I can tell that's the way it was Ma. If you look close, there does seem to be a slight resemblance to the Indians in our faces. Especially, the hooked nose on most of the men."

Sam was wide-eyed with wonder. "You mean my Great Grandma was a full blooded Cherokee! Does that mean she was royal blood cause she was a chief's daughter?"

Alonzo laughed, "I reckon it does. Ain't that something? We've got royal blood flowin' in our veins."

"Shaw!" Susie said. She clearly disapproved of this twist to the family history.

The horses were hardy animals, but it was necessary to stop and give them a rest periodically. The rest stop was near water when possible, so that the horses could drink as well as the family.

Bridges were a luxury that was missing at most stream crossings, so the stream had to be forded. Some were shallow enough that they presented no problem. Others required the horses to swim and the wagon to float.

The children were fond of jumping off, rolling up their pants legs, and wading through the stream when it wasn't too deep. Often, wet clothes were the result.

The noon stop was near Bullard's Creek. Gus dismounted from the wagon and tied the horses to a low branch of a tree while Alonzo helped Susie down. The family would have their midday meal, rest a while, and move on during the afternoon. Alonzo usually carried some fishing line. Today was no exception. He cut a small sprout of a tree to use as a pole. Some digging in nearby wet soil yielded a number of earthworms. He then proceeded to fish for some of the small pan fish which were so abundant in the small creek. Susie spread out a quilt on the ground. Gus helped her bring the lunch basket and spread the family picnic. After lunch the children, who were full of energy, were restless.

"Ma, can we go swimmin'?" Tom asked.

"I don't think so. We've got be goin'."

"Please! Ma."

"Ask your Pa."

"How about it, Pa?"

Alonzo looked thoughtful for a bit, grinned and said, "Okay, just for a little while."

The younger children stripped down to their underwear and went splashing into the creek. Alonzo moved upstream to try his fishing where there was less noise.

Some time later, he returned with a dozen small pan fish. "These'll help at supper," he said.

The fish were cleaned and placed in a bucket of water to keep them from spoiling. By now, the younger children had worn themselves out playing in the water and were ready to sleep for awhile.

The journey resumed with the children fast asleep in the wagon bed and Alonzo and Susie seated on the wagon seat. Gus and Sam had decided to walk for a while, so they trailed along behind the wagon.

About the middle of the afternoon, they arrived at the Hall farm located in the Altamaha district of Jeff Davis County. The Hall family owned what would have been considered a plantation in former times, but was now mostly a large tract of land worked by the family and several hired hands.

This family had a proud tradition and was highly influential in the community as well as the county and state. The patriarch of the family was Sebastian Hall, better known as Sebe, who had signed the Articles of Secession of the Confederacy, representing the County of Appling for the State of Georgia.

Sebe was welcoming each family as they arrived. Rather spry for a man in his 80's, he would wave as they approached the house. Alonzo stopped near the front of the house to speak.

"Hello, Uncle Sebe. How've you been?"

"Tol'able, tol'able, for an old coot like me, Alonzo."

"Old! Heck, you'll outlive us all. They'll have to call you up at the judgement and knock you in the head."

"I doubt it. These old bones ache a lot now-a-days. Just don't have the spit I used to."

"Well, it's good to see you, anyway. Where do you want us to park this rig?"

"Just find you a spot in the shade anywhere and put your horses in the lot. There's plenty of fodder and corn for everybody."

The family set up camp under the shade of a large oak tree. Gus unhitched the team and led them away to feed and water while the others unpacked the wagon. Alonzo cleared the wagon bed and ran a couple of bows over the top to hold his tarp in place. He and Susie would sleep in the wagon bed, the smaller children underneath the wagon, and the others would lay out pallets under the tree.

Sam was assigned the task of gathering wood from the wood pile and starting the fire. The job done, he could now go about finding something else to occupy his time.

Susie set up her cooking utensils and soon had supper cooking. She made use of the fresh fish Alonzo had caught and prepared a good variety of other dishes.

After supper, the family moved to the patio located at the rear of the farm house where a dance was traditionally held during the family reunion. Alonzo and Susie weren't too keen on dancing, but they wanted to join in the conversation, and that was where everybody was.

The band consisted of a banjo, fiddle, and guitar. Mostly young couples were dancing to the music, but a few older couples joined in too.

Gus danced a couple of dances with two of the young women and retired to the refreshments to get something to drink. As he filled his cup at the punch bowl, he looked up and saw what he thought was the reddest head of hair he had ever seen. She must have been in her late teens, and she was looking at him with an impish grin, almost a flirt.

Eva and Estell Hester had been watching him from across the dance floor. Estell had said, "I dare you to walk up to him and introduce yourself." That was all it took to spur Eva into action. She had little qualms about what a proper young lady would do.

"Hello, I'm Eva. What's your name?"

"I'm Gus. Gus Reynolds," Gus said, with just a bit of hesitation.

Eva smiled at him and said, "I believe you know my brother, George."

"George?"

"George Hester."

"You're George Hester's sister?"

"That's right. He made a trip with you on the river last spring."

The surprise in Gus's voice subsided as he said, "It's nice to meet you. Would you like to dance?"

Eva gave a slight curtsey, as her mother had taught her, and answered, "I'd be delighted to."

Eva allowed Gus to lead her on to the dance floor and they danced through one set. When the band paused, Gus said, "Let's set a spell."

They found a seat on the edge of the crowd and caught their breath. Gus said, "That's the most dancing I've done in awhile."

Eva sighed and said, "Me too. I sure could use some of that punch."

Gus stood and said, "Stay right here, I'll fetch it."

As soon as Gus was gone, Estell was by Eva's side. "I didn't think you'd do it."

Eva looked away from her sister and sighed. "He's just about the handsomest man I've ever seen. There's no way I'm going to miss the chance to meet him. Now get lost before he comes back. I want him all to myself for awhile."

"Okay, let me know how it goes."

Gus returned carrying two glasses of punch. He handed one to Eva, sipped from the other, and said, "This is just about the most beautiful night I've ever seen. Ain't that moon pretty?"

"Yes. I've dreamed about nights like this," Eva said, with a sigh in her voice.

Gus finished his glass of punch, placed the empty glass on a tray, and asked, "Would you care to dance again?"

"I don't think so."

"What would you like to do?"

"Something exciting."

"Like what?"

"You think of something."

"How about a stroll?"

"I thought you'd never ask."

Gus and Eva slipped away from the crowd and walked around the house and down the lane. The harvest moon shown through the trees casting sculptured shadows in the night. The stars were bright points of light in the ink dark sky. Crickets chirped merrily in the evening breeze.

"Where do you live?" Gus asked.

"Oh, not too far from here. Over close to Crossroads Church."

"That's not far at all," Gus said, carefully. He wanted to sound as good as he could. First impressions were very important, especially with someone you wanted to impress.

"Do you always come the night before the reunion dinner?" Gus inquired.

"Mostly. Pa plays banjo in the band, so we come early and spend the night before the reunion."

"Oh, so your Pa's a musician."

"Yes. He plays for lots of dances all over this part of the county."

"Do you go to a lot of dances?"

"Not many. Pa says most of the places he plays ain't fit for young ladies."

"Oh, I see. Do you dance a lot at home?"

"Most of the family enjoys music and dancing. You know, almost any excuse to have a party."

Gus and Eva had reached the end of the lane and the country road was before them. "I guess we'd better head back toward the house," Gus suggested.

"Yes. If I'm gone too long, Ma'll send somebody looking for me."

The couple made their way back up the lane continuing their casual conversation until they reached the front of the house. Estell was there, almost in a tizzy. "Where have you been?" she demanded. "Ma's started to lookin' for you."

Eva looked at her defiantly. "We're just talkin'."

"If Ma finds out, you'll be in trouble," Estell challenged.

Gus felt caught in the middle. "Maybe I should just say good night."

Eva looked at him and sighed. "That'd probably be best. We don't want to rile Ma."

Gus reached and took her hand. It was soft and warm and small in his own. "Maybe we could talk some more tomorrow."

Eva gave the slightest hint of a smile. "I'd like that."

"Good night. I enjoyed our talk," Gus said, as he gripped her hand, then released it and walked away.

As Gus departed, Eva turned on Estell. "What do you mean buttin' in?" she demanded in her best fit of red-haired temper. "We were just gettin' acquainted."

"You know you'll catch it if Ma finds you walking in the moonlight with him. She'd say it ain't proper for a young lady to go strollin' off in the night like that."

"Mind your own business. You ain't my Ma!"

* * *

Gus decided not to return to the dance. Instead, he walked back to the family's camp site and sat down by the tree. He was all alone. The others were still at the dance or chatting somewhere.

He lay back and tried to relax, but his head was filled with thoughts of the fiery red-head he had just encountered. It was hard to explain, but there was something different about her. He felt warm inside when he pictured her and remembered her smile and defiant temper. This was a girl he would like to get to know better.

Other family members returned to the camp eventually and everyone bedded down for sleep. Sam joined Gus out under the tree, and Tom decided to sleep there, too.

* * *

Gus awoke with a start. That cussed rooster was crowing his fool head off. Didn't he have sense enough to know he couldn't bring the sun up? The one morning he could sleep late and that confounded chicken wouldn't shut up.

Once awake, Gus decided to get up and go feed and water the animals. At the stables, he found everything he needed to care for the horses. They must be well fed, since they would have a long day ahead. The family would leave soon after dinner and make their way home, arriving late in the night.

By the time Gus returned, Susie was busy fixing breakfast. "Sam, go fetch me another bucket of water," Susie ordered.

"Yes'em." Sam hurried off to obey.

"Gus, would you spread the table cloth?" Susie asked.

The rest of the family sat down to breakfast, but Susie continued to cook over the campfire coals. She was going to be sure she made her fair share of vittles for the reunion dinner.

One could have questioned if all Susie's preparation was necessary. The Hall family had been cooking for two days. A barbecue topped off a feast of almost any dish the Southern cook's mind could conceive.

Gus shaved and dressed in his best suit for the dinner. He

wanted to look his best for Eva.

Susie assigned everybody a task, and soon the food was on its way to the big table to be placed with food from other families. Gus placed his burden on the table and looked around. He had never seen so much food in his life. If anybody went away hungry from this table, it would be their own fault.

Latecomers were arriving now. Several families had waited until morning to make the short trip from their nearby homes. This was a major social event, so friends and neighbors were invited. Many of them arrived at the last minute.

Gus looked for Eva among the milling crowd, hoping to catch a glimpse of her, and maybe talk to her again. Finally, he caught sight of her carrying a tray of food. She was wearing a bright green dress with a long flowing skirt that almost swept the ground as she walked. Her red hair cascaded down over her shoulders and contrasted beautifully with the green of the dress.

Gus watched her from afar as she placed the tray on the table and began to rearrange dishes. Eva turned and saw him watching her. She did not respond, but moving off to the side of the crowd, she glanced aside to see if he was looking.

Gus took the hint and followed her. Just as she rounded the corner of the house he caught up to her. "Well, good morning," he said.

"Good morning, yourself. Do you always stare at people?"

"Just on special occasions."

"What occasions?"

"When they're nice to look at," Gus smiled.

Eva decided she liked his smile too, but she said, "Ma says it ain't polite to stare at folks."

"Nobody ever accused me of bein' polite. Why don't we have dinner together?"

"I don't know. If Ma sees us she might give me the devil."

"Why don't you introduce me to your Ma? Then we can get to know one another properly."

Eva looked at Gus with exasperation, "You don't know my Ma."

"I will after we meet each other."

"Well, okay," Eva conceded.

* * *

Sebe Hall was trying to get everyone's attention. "May I have your attention! It's certainly good to see you here for this special occasion. We trust everybody had a good trip and hope you are enjoyin' yourself. We're about to eat, so let's gather round and ask Pastor Thompkins to bless the food."

Thompkins stood up and removed his hat, placing it over his heart,he began the blessing. He ain't hungry, Gus thought after Thompkins had been praying for a minute or more. Finally, the blessing was over and the crowd began to file past the table and load their plates.

Gus and Eva fixed plates and found seats under the shade of a nearby oak. They ate in silence for a while. "Do you mind if I come callin'?" Gus asked.

"I don't mind, but we have to ask Ma and Pa."

"We'll take care of that soon," Gus assured her.

Gus finished his food and reached for his drink. Eva said, "I didn't get any dessert. Come on, let's go get some of that thin-layer chocolate cake."

Gus followed Eva as she made her way toward the table. He almost ran into her as she stopped dead in her tracks. Her mother was sitting there. Eva felt like the cat that swallowed the canary, but she recovered quickly. "Ma, I'd like you to meet Gus."

Annie Hester looked Gus over with a critical eye and inquired, "Are you Alonzo Reynolds's boy?"

Gus smiled and tipped his hat, "Yes, ma'am."

"Ma, Gus would like to come callin'. That is, if it's okay."

"You'll have to ask your Pa about that, young lady."

Eva almost breathed a sigh of relief. That would be the easy part. She had always been able to talk Pa into almost anything she wanted. She said, "We'll go talk to Pa then."

"Nice to meet you, ma'am," Gus said, as he and Eva walked away.

"Your Ma just don't know me yet," Gus encouraged Eva.

"Ma ain't likely to like anybody who wants to court me," Eva returned.

There were so many desserts to choose from that Gus and Eva finally settled on two each and returned to their place at the table. Gus ate one of his desserts and paused. "Don't you think we should talk to your Pa?"

"Don't worry about Pa. I'll handle him."

"Okay, if you say so."

When the meal was over, there were speeches by different heads of families. Gus and Eva sat together and listened but were not really interested. Both wanted to get away by themselves for a while.

Finally, the gathering was over, and those who had long distances to travel began packing and leaving one by one. The Reynolds family had as far to go as anyone so they were among the first to leave.

Gus and Eva had to say goodbye, but they each did it reluctantly. "When will I see you again?" Eva asked.

"I'm going to Lumber City in a few days. How would it be if I stopped by on my way?"

"That'd be fine. What're you goin' there for?"

"I'll be workin' a loggin' camp there for the winter. Might be, I can get back sometime."

"That's good."

Gus took Eva's hands in his and held them firmly. "I've really enjoyed meetin' you, Eva. I'll be lookin' forward to the next time."

Eva smiled, "So have I, Gus. I'll be watchin' for you."

Gus turned and followed the family wagon as it moved down the lane. He looked back and waved one last time. As he gazed at Eva, he wondered what her lips would taste like. But that would have to wait for another time.

Estell approached Eva as she stood looking after the wagon as it kicked up dust down the lane. "Is it safe to talk to you now?"

Eva stood still, watching the departing wagon. She said to herself, but loud enough for Estell to hear, "Gus Reynolds doesn't know it, but I'm goin' to marry him someday."

Chapter 4
Logging Camp

The cool winds of Autumn were blowing. It was now October and the leaves were turning their varied shades of color and falling from the trees. Warm days would sometime break the trend, but for the most part winter steadily approached and would soon claim its reign over the land.

Most of the farm work could now be carried on by the younger sons, so Gus made preparation to leave for his winter work in the logging camps. He packed a bedroll with those essentials he needed to survive the coming winter cold. Warm clothing was a must if one were to survive the often hostile environment of the swamps.

"Gus," Susie called from the hallway, "Did you remember to pack the new pair of long underwear I got you?"

"Yes, Ma."

"Don't forget to carry that winter jacket."

"I won't."

Gus finished his pack, tied it securely, and slung it over his shoulder as he stepped into the hallway. Susie, always concerned that he didn't eat enough, handed him a small cloth bag with a drawstring.

"Here's some food for the trip."

"Thanks, Ma."

"Let us hear from you. I worry about you off up there in that loggin' camp."

"I'll be all right, Ma," Gus said, as he reached for the bag and gave her a hug with his free arm.

"Try to come visit some during the winter."

"I will, Ma."

Gus turned and walked out the door, down the steps, and into the morning light.

If you were affluent, you could ride a train, or maybe ride a horse when you traveled long distances. Gus was not affluent by any stretch of the imagination, so he walked. His trail was the same as that followed by the family to the Hall Plantation. He then proceeded to travel west until he reached Cross Roads Community. As he passed Cross Roads Church, a winding sandy road led to the top of a hill about a half mile from the Church.

Nestled back among pecan trees at the top of the hill, sat the rambling family home of the Hester family. As Gus approached the house, he could see what remained of several flower beds. The cool weather had begun to take its toll on the flowers, but some winter plants still showed signs of nature's beauty.

Standing at the gate, Gus hailed the house where lights had just been lit to ward off the coming darkness. "Hello! Anybody home?"

Footsteps echoed down the central hallway of the house and a male voice asked, "Who is it?"

"Gus, Gus Reynolds."

"Oh. Yes. Now I remember. Eva said you'd be callin'," Bill Hester said, as he extended his hand in greeting.

"Sir, I know I didn't ask you before, but I'd like to see Eva, if you don't mind."

"I reckon that'd be all right. We were just fixin' to eat supper. Won't you come in and join us?"

"Thank you."

Gus followed Bill down the hallway of the house, across the breezeway, and into the warm kitchen. The smell of a warm meal greeted him as he entered.

The invitation of a person to a meal at the last minute was not unusual. It was common practice to prepare more food than required by the family. Common courtesy required that no one be left out, no matter how large or meager the fare.

"Look who's here," Bill announced as they moved to the dining table.

Gus responded to the various greetings and seated himself at the table as Bill motioned him to a place. The family said grace and began the meal. Meanwhile Eva, who was seated across the table from Gus, had not said a word except to acknowledge Gus's greeting.

The usual chatter accompanied the meal and when everyone had finished, Annie said, "Why don't you men go to the sitting room? Me and the girls will join you as soon as we do the dishes."

Gus joined Bill and his sons in the sitting room and they chatted about farming and other incidental subjects. After some time, the ladies joined them. "Pa, how about playing us a tune?" Estell suggested.

One of the boys soon returned with Bill's banjo and the music began. Gus took turns dancing with the ladies. Finally, it was his turn to dance with Eva. They did a polka together and then retired to the settee. Under the watchful eye of Ma and Pa, they sat and talked.

"I didn't know exactly when you were comin'," Eva said.

"I wasn't sure myself. Things were kind of uncertain."

"Are you on your way to Lumber City?"

"Yes. I'm supposed to be there tomorrow or the next day."

"Where're you stayin' tonight?"

"I'll probably camp somewhere on the road."

"It's awfully cold to sleep outside, ain't it?"

"I've slept in worse."

"Maybe Pa'd let you sleep in our barn. It ain't much, but it's better than nothin'."

"I don't want to be any trouble."

"It won't be no trouble. I'll ask Pa."

Eva rose and stepped over to Bill, who was picking another verse of "Soldier's Joy," and whispered in his ear. Bill nodded his head in agreement with her suggestion as he continued to play the banjo.

After what seemed a long time, Bill laid his banjo aside, stretched and yawned, and said, "I'm bushed. This has been a long day. We'd all best get some rest." Turning to Gus, he said, "Why don't you spend the night with us, young man? We've kinda got a full house, but you're welcome to sleep in the barn if you're so inclined."

Gus stood and acknowledged the offer, "Thank you, sir. I was plannin' to bed down on the road, but a warm place would sure be nice."

"It's settled then. Eva, why don't you show our guest to the barn?"

Annie looked at Bill with a disapproving glance, but said nothing. After Gus and Eva left, Bill turned to her and said, "Now, Ma, they ain't gonna have time to get into no mischief. 'Sides they need a bit of time alone."

Gus retrieved his bedroll and followed Eva into the night. They exited the house by the front door and walked through the pecan grove to the barn behind the house. Eva opened the barn door and shined the lantern inside. They entered the barn just before a gust of wind blew the door shut. Eva hung the lantern on a nail that had been driven there for that purpose.

Turning to face Gus, she said, "I hope you'll be comfortable."

"I'll be just fine."

"I'd best hurry back to the house. You can keep the light if you want."

"Thank you, but before you go I'd like to know something."

"What?"

Gus reached for her hands and pulled her closer to him. He could feel the warmth of her body and smell the fresh scent of her hair. Eva didn't resist as he brought his face to hers and kissed her fully on the lips. He drew back and said, "I've been wondering what that would be like ever since we met at the reunion."

Eva smiled, "Well, how was it?"

"Just as nice as I'd imagined."

Eva suddenly remembered where she was and said, "I'll have to go now. Will I see you in the mornin'?"

"I can stay for awhile."

"Good. Why don't you have breakfast with us?"

"If you insist."

"I insist. Good night," Eva said, as she ran from the barn into the night.

Gus scattered some hay, spread his bedroll over it, and lay down to sleep. He dozed off to sleep, savoring the taste of Eva's kiss on his lips, and dreamed pleasant dreams.

* * *

The next day dawned bright and cold. There was a slight frost covering the fields as Gus rose from his bed of hay and prepared to face the day. He packed his bedroll and went to the house for breakfast.

After the meal, Gus said goodbye to the rest of the family as he and Eva walked together to the front gate. Gus shifted his bedroll to his shoulder, straightened his hat, and said, "I'll have to be goin' now, but I'll see you again soon. I'll be back this way ever' time I run a raft down river."

Eva smiled, and taking his hand said, "I'll be expecting you most any time. Goodbye."

Gus turned and walked down the lane toward Hazlehurst, the winding road taking him past fields yet to be harvested and woods filled with beautiful virgin timber.

* * *

Hazlehurst was another muddy little town near the railroad, much like Baxley, with possibly a little smaller population. Gus walked into town about mid-morning and proceeded down the wagon road near the railroad tracks heading northwest toward Lumber City. He still had some seven miles to complete his trek. The traffic on the road was sparse, but a farm wagon overtook him and the driver was kind enough to give him a ride.

When they reached the river, Gus left the farmer to continue by ferry while he walked westward along the river to the camp. The trails were even more difficult in the swamps. The roads, if you could call them roads, were deep rutted where ox carts had been driven through the mud and water. The ruts were often filled with water and the oxpath was the best place to walk, if you didn't mind walking through cow manure.

Gus reached the logging camp late in the afternoon. As he

approached the camp, several men milled about taking care of equipment. He decided to inquire for the camp boss. "Howdy, where do I find the boss?"

An older man with a gray beard spat tobacco juice on the muddy ground and answered, "He's down to the tent, I think."

"Thanks," Gus said, as he continued down the muddy trail.

The tent served as headquarters for the logging operation. Here the foreman kept track of the men and payroll and other business items necessary for the timber work.

"Hello! Anybody here?" Gus called.

"Just a minit," a voice answered from inside the tent.

A tall man wearing a battered hat stooped and emerged from the tent flap. Straightening himself, he inquired, "What can I do for you?"

"I'm looking for Ray Hall. I understand he's timber boss here."

"I'm Hall. Who're you?"

"Gus Reynolds. Your new raft pilot."

"Oh, yeah. I didn't expect you till tomorrow."

"I decided to make it a day early. Didn't see any need to sit on my butt for one more day."

"That's good. We can use ever' hand we can get. Old man Fletcher wants all the work done yesterday."

"Where do I hang my hat?"

"Just stow your gear in the shed down the hill."

Gus moved on in the direction indicated by Hall. The shed was a temporary structure built of poles and palmetto leaves. It served as sleeping quarters for the logging crew and was fairly dry, except in heavy rains.

Gus stowed his sleeping bag against the back wall in an empty space and looked around for the cook shed. It lay about twenty-five yards uphill. The cook was ringing a bell to let the hands know that supper was ready.

A logging camp is not a family environment, and the language and behavior of its men would not be approved of in any Sunday School. The men crowded around the cook fires and filled the plates and wolfed their food down without the benefit of any such formalities as a blessing or even washing their hands. Gus waited for the crowding to subside, filled a plate with beans and bread, poured a cup of coffee, and sat on a log to eat his meal.

There was a code among men who labored in such camps that any newcomer had to fight the toughest man in camp. Usually, there was always someone who felt he fit this description and had to maintain his reputation. Gus was not unaware of this tradition, so he was not surprised when the incident occurred.

A towering hunk of a man, known among the loggers simply as Bull, approached Gus after the meal. Bull wasted no time on amenities. Gus stood to meet him as he approached.

Bull looked at Gus with a leer on his face and challenged, "What's yore name, stranger?"

Gus looked him square in the eye and replied evenly, "Gus."

"Well, ain't you a pretty sight? Boys, he's clean shaved and wearing clean clothes. You don't look like no logger to me," Bull spat on the ground.

Gus watched him carefully and answered the challenge, "Maybe you'd like to dirty me up some so I'll be as pretty as you."

"Maybe I will," Bull breathed as he swung his right fist at Gus with a hay-making swing.

Gus stepped back and the blow went harmlessly by his chest. Bull recovered and followed through with a left hook. This blow connected with Gus's right shoulder and sent him against a log. Rolling to miss the kick that Bull followed through with, Gus was on his feet like a cat.

Bull was a big man and, like most big men, depended on his great strength to finish his opponent. But Gus was quicker and more agile. Consequently, he could attack and retreat fast enough to score a blow more frequently.

Bull attempted to kick Gus in the groin, but Gus saw it coming and intercepted the kick with his hands, twisting the foot so that Bull fell sideways into the mud. Bull rolled over and came up cussing as he charged Gus in an attempt to lock him in a bear hug. Gus side-stepped the charge and delivered a right into the pit of Bull's stomach. As Bull doubled over in pain, Gus hit him behind the neck with his left hand. Bull fell like a ton of brick and lay groaning in the mud.

Gus sat on a log and hassled for breath. His body ached from the blows it had taken and his head pounded as the blood rushed through it. He knew he would be sore all over tomorrow, but that couldn't be helped.

Everybody had been watching the fight and now stood looking as the two men recovered from their exertion. Finally, Bull rolled over and sat up rubbing the back of his neck. "Damned if you don't pack a mean rabbit punch, Mister."

Gus just looked at him for a minute. Nobody said anything. Then Gus said, "If you've had enough, I'll manage."

Bull raised himself from the ground and sat beside Gus on the log, "I'm satisfied," he said, with a grin.

A cheer went up from the spectators as they realized the conflict was over. Gus had proven to them he wasn't afraid to face a challenge.

* * *

Logging was extremely hard work, and you had to be tough to survive. Trees were felled by sawing them with crosscut saws. Two men, one on each handle, would saw partially through the trunk of the tree, chop a notch with an axe, and fell the tree by completing the cut through the remaining trunk from the opposite side. This operation would sometimes take as much as a half day, depending on the size of the trunk.

The trees were then limbed and cut into convenient lengths for handling. The size lumber needed also determined the lengths. These logs were then gathered together to form piles called "brows."

A team of oxen pulling a timber cart was used to accomplish the moving task. The timber cart was a two-wheel wagon device consisting of two high wheels at least six feet tall. Fastened to a sturdy axle between the wheels was a short chain with a set of hooks.

The cart driver would position the cart over the log. Unhooking the trace chains from the oxen, he would then raise the tongue of the cart until the hooks gripped the log. Reattaching the trace chains to the raised tongue, he would then drive the oxen forward thus raising the log. Forward motion kept the end of the log off the ground and made it easier for the oxen to pull their load. Once at the brow, the logs were rolled into piles by means of poles and a tool called a "cant-hook," a device consisting of a handle about four feet long with a hook attached to one side with a hinge.

Whenever possible, the brow was located on a slope where the logs could be rolled into the river. They were then fastened with ropes and/or poles and spikes to form raft sections. Rafts could be formed in as many sections as the pilot felt he could successfully steer on the river.

Rafting was usually done when waters were at their highest. Low water could present a problem because of sandbars and other obstructions in the river. Ordinarily, the water was low in the fall in South Georgia, so a raft pilot usually worked in the timber harvest until the waters began to rise from the winter and spring rains.

Gus labored alongside the regular loggers felling trees, topping them, and occasionally driving the oxen. A man might have a specialty, but when you worked timber, you pretty well had to be a jack-of-all-trades.

Snakes were a frequent threat to loggers. Mostly, snakes avoid humans. So if you follow the same trail through the woods you don't encounter one very often. But when you are constantly working new woods, as in timber harvest, meetings are almost inevitable.

There are three types of poisonous snakes found in South Georgia. The most common is the rattlesnake, of which there are two varieties, the timber rattler and the more famous diamond-back. Cottonmouths are also found near streams. The coral snake is also present, but less common.

Snakes usually hibernate for the winter. Being cold blooded

creatures, they become sluggish at temperatures below 40°
Fahrenheit. However, daylight temperatures sometimes reach
levels that enable them to be active. An operation such as logging
also uncovers the snake's den.

Unknown to Gus and Tom Morris, a diamond back rattler
had found a place underneath a log they were about to move. As
they approached to hookup, he made no sound. Tom was
preparing to set the hooks on the log when the rattler sounded a
warning buzz of its rattlers. Tom tried to dodge, but he couldn't
tell exactly where the snake lay. The rattler's fangs penetrated the
cloth of his shirt sleeve and found their mark in his left forearm.

Gus often carried a 38 caliber pistol strapped to his left side
for just such an emergency. Drawing the pistol cross-handed, he
fired before the snake could recoil to strike again. The bullet tore
the snake's head from its body. It lay writhing on the ground.

Tom was feeling the adrenalin flow as he staggered back
against the log. "The son-of-a-bitch got me, Gus!"

"Don't move!"

Gus snatched his bandanna from around his neck and
fashioned a tourniquet above Tom's elbow. Retrieving a pocket
knife from his right front pocket, Gus cut the shirt sleeve until he
could see the fang marks.

"This may hurt a bit," Gus said, as he cut through the fang
marks with the blade of his knife. Tom gritted his teeth. An x
across each mark allowed the blood to flow freely from the
wound. Placing his mouth over the cuts, Gus sucked the poisoned
blood from the wound and spat on the ground. The tourniquet
was then loosened temporarily so that blood could reach the
forearm briefly.

Gus gathered Tom in his arms and carried him to the camp.
Excitement began to build as the loggers realized what had
happened. Placing Tom under the lean-to, Gus propped his head
on a blanket and elevated the arm to minimize the blood flow to
the forearm. "Don't try to be tough," Gus said.

"Thanks," Tom sighed.

"Anybody got any whiskey?" Gus asked of the men who had

gathered by this time.

Nobody said anything, but someone left and returned with a small flask. Gus handed the flask to Tom. "Here, drink as much of this as you can. The pain's going to be hell in a little while and the less you feel the better."

This treatment would probably be considered all wrong by modern medicine, but doctors were simply not available and would have likely treated the patient in much the same way. A surprising number of snake bite victims survived in spite of the primitive treatment.

Tom was delirious for several hours. Gus would check him frequently, feeling his forehead for an increase in body temperature. Finally, the fever began to break.

Tom opened his eyes as Gus touched his face. "How you feelin?" Gus inquired.

"Like hell, to be honest with you," Tom said, weakly.

"Could you eat something?"

"I don't know. Maybe some liquid. My mouth's dry as cotton."

Gus returned with a broth the cook had prepared. "Here, try some of this dishwater," Gus grinned.

"You had me worried there for awhile. I thought I was gonna lose my best working partner."

"Thanks to you, I might just make it."

Tom finished the broth and closed his eyes. Gus eased away. As he relaxed, Tom went back to sleep. The rest was the best thing for him.

The next day, Gus made preparations to take Tom out of the swamp. He told Ray Hall he would need a wagon. Ray agreed, and Gus was on his way with Tom lying on the floor of the wagon. The trip to the Lumber City ferry took some time. The trail was rough, and Gus didn't want to jostle Tom too much.

Once they reached the ferry, Gus paid the fare for Tom and himself leaving the animals and wagon on the riverside. It would have cost him a great deal more to ferry the mules and wagon across the river twice. He needed the money to pay Tom's train fare home.

Helping Tom on board the ferry boat, Gus seated him on a barrel and stayed nearby as the ferryman worked them across the Ocmulgee River to the Lumber City landing. Once on the landing, Gus supported Tom for the half-mile or so to the depot where he purchased a ticket for him.

When the train arrived, Gus helped Tom aboard and spoke to the conductor with him. "This man's been snake-bit, and he's kind of weak. He needs to get off in Baxley. Can you help him and see that he gets home?"

The conductor looked at Tom, who was pale and sweating from the exertion of boarding the train. "Sure. Does anybody know he's comin'?"

"I'm sending a telegram to his folks as soon as I get off the train. Somebody ought to be there to meet him when you arrive."

"Okay. I'll see he gets where he's goin'."

Gus turned to Tom, "You take it easy now. I'll be seein' you soon. I don't want to lose my best workin' partner."

Tom grinned, "I'll do my best. Don't take no wooden nickels."

As the train pulled away from the station, Gus stepped to the telegrapher's window, reached for a pad and wrote a short message, handed the paper to the messenger and said, "How much?"

The telegrapher counted the words, scratched out one or two and said, "Fifty cents."

In the distance, the train whistle sounded for the river trestle and echoed down the river, giving off a mournful wailing sound. Gus watched as the train crossed the river and disappeared from sight. He had done all he could for Tom. He surely hoped it was enough.

Chapter 5
The Storm

December brought the rains. Rain was both a blessing and a curse for the loggers. A blessing because they needed the higher waters to get their trees to market. A curse because the inclement weather forced the workers to abandon their task for days at a time while the waters poured out of the sky, as a cold front would sweep across the area depositing vast amounts of liquid.

During these periods, the men would take refuge at the camp and attempt to stay as dry as possible under make-shift shelters, with roaring log fires to keep them warm and dry. After days of prolonged rainfall, the woods were too wet to work, so the hands would often take a furlough from their job and return to friends and family.

About two weeks into December, the rains began in earnest. Rain had been falling for three days. The ground was already soaked from torrential rains, so working in the mire was almost impossible. Gus took advantage of this time to return home for a visit and also find a way to visit Eva.

Gus, along with several of the men, walked out from the logging camp to the Lumber City ferry. Crossing the river they caught the train, because the rains continued to fall, and made their way to their various destinations. Gus purchased a ticket to get him to Baxley and boarded the train in the middle of the afternoon.

Travel by train was more hazardous during rainy weather due to flooding and weakened trestles and road beds. Fortunately, there were no washed-out bridges so the train was able to reach Baxley in about the normal time.

As Gus stepped down off the train in Baxley, it was evident that the rains had taken their toll on the local area as well. Baxley had been built near the railroad more than thirty years before. The building site had not been chosen because of the high ground. In fact, a number of natural ponds had to be drained in order to make it possible to build in many locations. The recent rains now flooded a major portion of the area.

Gus made his way between pools and mud-holes as best he could toward the center of main street, probably the highest point in town. Here a row of trees helped to soak the moisture from the ground. Also, watering troughs stood under trees and caught some of the overflow of rain.

Gus fully expected to have to slosh the five miles home through the rain and mud. Approaching the middle of the street, he spied a buggy that he thought he recognized.

"Well, I'll be damned if it ain't a duck!" Homer Youmans said.

Gus laughed, grinned good-naturedly, and said, "I've sure enough got webs between my toes, Uncle Homer. I see you ain't drowned yet."

"Nope. You on your way out to Alonzo's?"

"Sure am. You ain't goin' that way, are you?"

"It won't be out of the way none. I just got one more errand to attend to, if you don't mind waitin'."

"I'll wait a good while to keep from havin' to swim all the way."

"Hop aboard then."

Gus stepped up into the buggy as Homer spoke to his horse and moved across the street. A stop at the general store and Homer returned carrying a coker sack containing groceries, Gus presumed. Placing his burden under a tarp on the rear of the buggy, Homer mounted the vehicle and they moved north out of town toward the Reynolds' home.

The rain continued to fall, a fine mist coming down to add to the already saturated roads and fields. Ten-Mile Creek was swollen so that the buggy's axle dipped under the water as they forded it. A few more inches and the cargo on the back of the vehicle would have been wet.

A warm fire in the family home sent a column of smoke into the wet, chilly air as Homer and Gus pulled into the front yard.

"Uncle Homer, why don't you put your team and buggy under the shelter and come in for a cup of warm coffee? It's gettin' late. You might want to stay the night and go home in the mornin'," Gus offered.

"It's getting dark and I don't fancy crossin' some of them branches, as deep as they are, in the dark. I think I'll take you up on that, son."

Gus reached for the reins and said, "I'll unhitch the team and turn them in the stable. You go on in. Ma'll be glad to see you."

As Gus walked away with the team, Susie came to the front door. Looking out, she said, "Well, I'll be. Is that you, Homer? You're about the last person I'd expected to see tonight."

Homer grinned at his sister and said, as he stepped onto the porch, "Yep, it's me. Web feet and all."

"Where's your rig?"

"Gus is puttin' it up for me."

"Good Lord! Pa! Gus is home."

Alonzo met Homer and Susie as they came through the breezeway to the kitchen. Extending his hand, he said, "Homer, it's good to see you. What in the world brings you out on a night like this?"

"Well, I met Gus in town and he needed a ride, so I thought I'd accommodate him."

"You two come on to the kitchen. We ought to have some coffee that'll warm your innards," Susie said, as she hustled them down the walkway.

Gus came through the kitchen door carrying the coker sack from Homer's buggy. "Thought you might have somethin' in here the varmints would be attracted to," he said, placing the sack on the floor.

Homer acknowledged the favor with a nod of his head as he swallowed a draught of warm coffee, then said, "Thanks, there might be."

Susie handed Gus a cup of coffee. "It's good to have you home, son. How've you been? Did you get to see that nice girl you met at the reunion?"

Homer raised an eyebrow and winked at Gus. "Boy, you ain't gettin' serious are you?" he laughed.

Gus sipped his coffee, looked at the cup as if it were the most interesting object in the room, and said, "You can't never tell."

"Well, I'll be hanged. It's about time. Congratulations, boy."

"I'm not sure congratulations are in order. You see, I ain't asked her yet."

Homer shot Gus another grin, "Is she interested?"

"She's let me come callin' once. I think she might be."

"Well, you just keep on tryin'. I'll be looking forward to eatin' some cake."

Homer changed the subject, "Susie, you plannin' a big Christmas?"

"Lord! I don't reckon, Homer. How 'bout ya'll?"

"Nothing much, I reckon. Just thought we'd have a nice dinner with the family. If this flood don't let up, won't nobody be able to travel 'cept Noah in his ark."

"Homer! That's disrespectful and you know it," Susie scolded.

Alonzo interrupted, "I think I'll turn in. See you in the morning, Homer."

"Me, too," Gus added.

As Alonzo and Gus left the kitchen, Susie said, "Homer, you can sleep on the cot in Gus's room or here in the kitchen if you'd like."

Homer finished his cup of coffee and placed the cup on the dining table. "The kitchen will be fine, Sis."

"Okay, I'll leave you here then. I'll be right back with some covers."

Susie returned momentarily with two quilts and a pillow. She placed them on the floor and left the kitchen. Homer fixed himself a bed from the clothes and lay down for the night.

* * *

The next day dawned cloudy, but with less rain. The air began to take on more chill as north winds blew. This would be another cool, cloudy day.

Gus enjoyed being home with the family. He helped out with the chores and ran errands for his mother and father. It was also fun to play with the children and watch their antics. He began to think it might be nice to have his own children.

Christmas came. The family didn't make a big thing of Christmas. It was mostly another day and any gifts that were given were usually of a very practical nature--clothing, shoes and such. Gus had found time to get to town and buy his mother and Eva a gift. Susie would get hers Christmas, but Eva's would have to wait.

Finally, the weather began to clear. Gus was ready to get back to work. He wanted an excuse to see Eva, so he left a day early to return to Lumber City. He took his usual route through the forest to the Hester farm arriving early in the afternoon.

As he approached the house, he could see family members working in the yard and field. Eva was tending a flower-bed even though it was the beginning of winter. Her love of plants and flowers had been developed early and would continue to bless herself and others throughout her life time.

Eva was totally absorbed in her work and did not realize Gus was anywhere near until he spoke, as he stood behind her. "Good afternoon."

"Good grief! What do you mean sneakin' up on a body like that?" she gasped.

"I wanted to surprise you."

"You surprised me all right. You scared the livin' daylights out of me."

Eva stood and wiped her hand across her face to push back her flaming red hair. The action left a smudge of dirt on her face. She suddenly realized how she looked. "Good Lord! I look a mess."

Gus grinned, "I think you look beautiful."

"I'll just bet you do," Eva said, as she turned toward the house.

Gus followed her to the wash basin on the breezeway. She washed her face and hands, disappeared into the house and returned with a hair brush. Gus watched as she brushed her long red hair. He loved the way it fell over her shoulders creating a contrast with her plain cotton dress. When she had finished the task, she sat beside him on the step.

"Now that's better," Eva stated.

"I don't know. I kind of like girls with dirty faces."

"Pshaw! Don't give me that line. What you up to anyhow?"

"I took some time off for bad weather. I'm headed back to camp and thought I'd drop by and chat awhile. I found this, too. I thought I might give it to someone, if they would accept it," Gus said, as he pulled a small packet from his jacket pocket.

Eva's eyes lit up with anticipation. She was fond of presents and this one would be special. She wanted to reach out and take it from his hand, but restrained herself. "I might be able to help you find somebody that'd like it."

"I thought you might," Gus said, handing the packet to her.

Eva lost her restraint. She opened the packet hurriedly. As she completed unwrapping it, a necklace with a cameo pendant met her eyes.

"It's beautiful!"

"I thought you might like it."

"Like it! I love it," she said, softly caressing the gift.

"Here, allow me," Gus said, reaching for the necklace.

Unfastening the clasp, he placed the necklace around her neck and positioned the cameo squarely under her chin. As he leaned back, he pecked her on the cheek. Eva forgot her ladylike manners and returned the peck.

"Now, that's more like it," Gus said, as he admired the cameo against her sun-freckled skin.

"Thank you," Eva smiled.

Gus sat and admired Eva for another few seconds, then said, "I'll have to be goin'. Got to get back to Lumber City."

"Can't you stay for supper?"

"I'd like to, but your folks are gonna get tired of feedin' and housin' me."

"I don't think that's a problem."

"I don't want it to be."

"I'll ask Ma to set another plate, if you'll stay."

"I'd sure like an excuse to stay."

Eva grinned, "We'll think of something."

Gus remained for the evening meal, but hesitated to spend the night. Leaving soon after, he made his way to Lumber City by way of Hazlehurst.

* * *

Back at the logging camp, the pace had picked up. It was now possible to gather logs to form timber rafts. The loggers would roll five or six logs into a small stream, float them to the mouth of the stream, and bind them into rafts. Gus devoted most of his energy to forming rafts.

January came and with it another change in the weather. There is a saying in South Georgia, "If you don't like the weather, just wait a few hours, it will change." The old timers referred to this weather as a "Norther." Today, it would probably be called a "Siberian Express."

Clouds began to roll in from the northwest. This was normal since most weather systems came from this point of the compass. What made these different were the form of precipitation they left behind.

Gus and his crew were putting a small skiff of logs together when rain began to fall, almost sideways due to the force of the wind. The winds howled, reminding Gus of the tales he heard about witches and ghosts. As the winds increased in velocity, the temperature began to drop.

Gus finished tying the knot he had been working and said, "Boys, we'd better head for shelter. This one's gonna blow us away."

The men made their way through the driving rain to the

logging camp and into the best shelter they could find. A roaring fire helped add to the comfort of the lean-to and also helped dry their wet clothing. The shelter had been constructed so that the opening faced south, giving the men as much protection as possible from the onslaught of the north wind.

Slowly, the rain began to freeze as it fell before the gale force of the wind. Ice particles struck buildings, clothes, and skin, stinging, and then clinging, as the volume of precipitation continued to increase.

The animals turned their backs to the storm and huddled under trees in an attempt to shelter themselves. Gus knew that someone would have to check on them, so he asked a couple of the men to help him. They approached the corral and made sure the fence was secure. Then Gus had the men carry hay to the areas where they were huddled. There wasn't much chance the stock would try to eat during the storm, but they needed the food available just in case.

The cook had prepared a meal the best he could. The men gathered around and ate silently as the winds continued to howl through the trees, screaming like a banshee. Ray Hall decided he needed to say something to his crew.

"Boys, this one looks like it's gonna be a rough one. There's no time to get out of here, so we'll have to make do with what we have. I'd like each of you to pitch in and help secure the shelters as best you can. Food may be in short supply before we're through, so I'm going to ask you to ration our supplies. Charlie here will prepare a limited fare for the next few hours. If you don't have enough blankets and such, I've got a few spares in the company tent. Hang in there and help each other and we'll get through this just fine. Let's get busy."

After a few hours, the ice began to build up on the limbs and tree tops. Under this added weight, trees bowed and limbs split from even the sturdiest trees. The winds had subsided and now there was a steady, slow-falling, freezing rain mixed with sleet and small amounts of snow. One lean-to, situated under a large oak, crumpled under the weight of a falling limb.

Immediately, men from other areas leaped to the rescue of their fellow crew members, pulling the broken branches off and checking them for injuries. Fortunately, no one was seriously hurt. An attempt to repair the damage proved too difficult and the men abandoned the effort and moved the newly displaced men into the remaining shelters.

The men didn't talk much. They seemed to be conserving their strength for whatever emergency lay ahead. Everybody huddled under blankets to ward off the cold and wet. The fires were hot enough to dry the newly applied supply of wood. Steam rose from the edge of the flames as the heat evaporated the moisture from a log of firewood.

Night fell, and the onslaught of cold and freezing rain continued. The combination of weather and darkness gave the night an eerie sight and sound. You could hardly see your hand in front of your face except by the firelight. The sound of the incessantly falling rain and sleet made a monotonous dripping sound. The sounds could have been soothing, but not to men who were weathering a storm in make-shift shelters in the midst of a wet and dreary river swamp.

Gus wrapped himself in his winter jacket and his bed-roll and attempted to sleep. He had some success until the palmetto roof above his face began to drip. A drop of water descended squarely on his nose causing him to jerk awake with a startled movement. Cursing under his breath, he rolled over, pulled his bed roll over his head and tried to resume his rest.

The night was restless for everyone. Even the animals began to shuffle and complain as the freezing rain continued to accumulate on everything in sight. The temperature continued to drop. Finally, even the fires and covers were unable to keep the men warm. Gus's feet felt as if they were frozen. His hands were stiff from the cold and ice had begun to form on his outer clothing.

Day dawned without much change in the precipitation. There was now more light, but it was almost impossible to keep warm and dry. The men took turns warming themselves by rotating near the fire. In the bitter cold, it was almost impossible to tell when you were too close to the fire. More than one man's clothes were set on fire as he attempted to warm his freezing body. His fellows would shout, warning him of his plight and helping by dousing the fire on his clothing.

Charlie, the cook, prepared a meager breakfast and the crew ate silently. Most of them realized that more food would have helped them sustain the cold better, but surplus food was simply not available. Long term survival was the name of the game at this point in time.

Gus volunteered to check on the animals. Two other men went to help him. Most of them seemed to be okay, but one mule was down and appeared to be barely alive. Poor cuss probably won't make it through, Gus thought.

The storm continued through the day and the next night. Occasional lulls would raise the hopes of the crew, but a renewed surge of wind and increased precipitation dampened that hope.

Boredom began to overtake the men, and they talked more to relieve their boredom and their building tension. There's always someone in the crowd who wants to one-up everything and everybody. This crew was no exception.

"Why, I remember the winter of Ninety-three," said an old logger known as Boggs. "It was just about the worst winter you ever saw."

Ray looked at Boggs and decided to encourage him. After all, there wasn't anything else to do. "How bad was it, Boggs?"

"Well, sir, the wind blowed so hard that the ice and rain couldn't hit the ground. After while there was a solid sheet of ice about six feet off the ground held up by the wind."

Gus grinned, "It was that bad, uh?"

"Yep, you ain't never seed the like of it. Not only was the sheet of ice keepin' ever'body from moving 'round, the temperature dropped so low that the fire froze."

"That must of really been rough," someone chimed in.

"It shore was. It was nigh impossible to keep warm, what with that froze fire. But that froze fire sure came in handy later."

"How was that?" Ray asked.

"Well, you see, we cut off the tops of them flames and used 'em for torches to see how to get about at night."

"Oh, I see," Ray responded. "How long did them torches last?"

"Well, I buried one of them in my root cellar, and last time I dug it up it was still shining."

Everybody had a hearty laugh and others began to tell tall tales. Soon the mood was entirely changed and the men felt more optimistic about their present condition and their possible future.

On the third day, the storm broke. The precipitation had ceased, but the cold held sway. Time would tell how long it would take for the ice and snow cover to melt. Meanwhile the food supply was running low.

Ray asked for volunteers to cut trail to Lumber City and return for supplies. Gus volunteered, as did Jack and Bob.

"Take one of the wagons and a couple of oxen," Ray instructed. "We won't need 'em here for awhile."

One man drove the team while the other two broke trail for the oxen and wagon. The task was slow and laborious. Frequent rest stops were required. This type of weather was not common in South Georgia and the men were not equipped to handle this type of travel. Often, one of the trail leaders would break through the snow and ice into a hole too deep for the wagon, then a new trail had to be found. It's more difficult to follow, even a known trail, once it's covered by snow and ice.

Hours later, the trio reached the railroad and ferry. The ferry operator was across the river, so Gus signaled to him. Slowly, the ferry made its way across the river to them. Loading the wagon and team was the work of another few minutes. The return trip seemed a bit faster, probably because the men were nearer their destination.

A local general store supplied them with most of the supplies needed. Some of the items were in short supply, but the proprietor was as generous as he could be under the circumstances. After all, these loggers were good customers.

"Is there anything else I can get for you?" he asked.

"I reckon that'll do for now," Gus said, as he checked the supply list against the stack of goods. "Where can me and these boys get a bed for the night? That trail ain't gonna be fit to travel in the dark."

"I think Ma's Boarding house might have some beds. It's hard to tell with this bad weather."

"Thanks, we'll check it out."

Leaving their supplies to be picked up next morning, the trio sloshed down the street through the snow and ice to find a room. Luckily, Ma's had one room available.

"Could we maybe get a bath?" Gus questioned.

"I don't see why not," Ma Baker responded.

"I'd like the loan of a razor too, if you don't mind."

"One razor comin' up. Anything else?"

"I don't reckon."

A tub of warm water helped to wash the weariness out of Gus's bones. He simply sat and soaked himself.

"Hey, leave some of the heat in that water for us," Bob hollered.

"You might just have to get you another tub," Gus returned.

A bath and shave made Gus feel more human. The boarding house meal of meat, potatoes, biscuit and gravy didn't do his constitution any harm either.

As night fell, the temperatures plunged again. Gus hoped the trail would remain passable. A melted, then refrozen trail could prove to be worse than a fresh broken one. At least, the night sky was clear. The weather had finally broken. Maybe things were looking up for a change.

Gus, Bob, and Jack bedded down for the night. Gus let Jack and Bob have the bed while he spread a pallet on the floor. He didn't want to become too accustomed to the soft life. After all, tomorrow was another hard day. Anyway, he liked a firm bed.

Gus slept soundly and dreamed of a beautiful red-haired woman. He'd have to do something about making her his wife in the not too distant future.

Chapter 6
Wild River

The return trip to camp from Lumber City was accomplished with some difficulty, but the trail remained open and the wagon could pass. Arriving at camp, Gus and his crew reported to Ray and then unloaded their precious cargo into the supply shed.

The world began to thaw and work began again, as the pace became more hectic in preparation for shipping the timber to market. Gus's duties now consisted of managing the construction of several rafts. He would pilot a lead raft, others would follow as the first flotilla of logs went to market.

"Boys, make sure those ropes are tight," Gus coached as he supervised the construction of his lead raft.

These rafts were being tied together with ropes initially. Then small timbers would be used to bind them together by drilling holes in outer logs with a tool called an "augur." The front section of the raft would have a bow, of sorts, about six feet across at the front. This bow would then slope back until the raft was about 25 feet wide. Additional sections of timber were attached to the bow by means of iron hooks called "dogs." A common size full raft was about 175 feet long containing 25,000 to 30,000 board feet of round timber.

Sturdy construction was vital. The river could sometimes be tricky and rafts would break apart causing not only loss of the timber, but on rare occasions, loss of life.

Gus checked a connection and then another. "This rig's got to cross some of the roughest water on the river, so make sure every joint's tight."

Ray had decided to send three rafts down river initially. Gus would pilot the lead raft and warn the others what lay ahead as they navigated the river to Darien. Each raft would carry a crew of three men. Afterward, Gus would be the main pilot making regular runs between the logging camp and the mill with a regular crew. By returning by train, the crew would be able to ship a raft about every ten days.

Gus decided to construct a shelter near the center of his raft. Various shapes were used from time to time by different raftsmen. Some of these were rather boxy and not very practical. Gus preferred a structure somewhat like an Indian tepee. It provided more space under the roof for storage and was easily made by tying poles together and wrapping them with a small tarp. The shape was also better suited for winds they might encounter. The fire pit was built near the front of the tepee so that heat from the fire would help keep the tent warm.

Finally, the initial preparations were complete and the crews were anxious to begin their voyages. Their eagerness had to be contained, however, because the work had been completed late in the afternoon and there was no moon tonight.

Early the next morning, the crews had their breakfast and prepared to cast off. Gus ran a double check of his raft and equipment. This was dangerous work, and you could lose your raft, not to mention your life, by carelessness.

"Okay, boys, let's put her in the channel," Gus called.

"Casting off bow line," Jack called.

"Casting off stern," Bob echoed.

"Man the oars," Gus ordered as he gave a heave on the bow sweep.

Slowly the huge lumbering craft began to move away from the riverbank as the current caught it and assisted the men as they manned their oars and pushed away from the hill with the hook'n jam poles. The raft rode low in the water and that made her a little harder to steer than usual, but no two rafts were alike and you had to learn to handle each one as you went along.

After some time the raft was near the main channel and moving down river with a good steady speed. Once in the channel, the main task was to steer the craft and keep it headed downstream.

The Ocmulgee River was high from the winter rains and the channel was deep. There was little risk of shallow water. The most difficult steering was on sharp bends of the river known as "points."

"Point comin' up, boys," Gus called. "Hold'er steady on the stern, and when I give the word, let me have all the leverage you got."

Gus pulled the bow sweep to try and guide the raft across the current so that the bow didn't turn too quickly. When the bow was a short distance from the approaching bank he began to steer the other direction. "Give me all you've got."

The big floating mass of timber moved as if in a dream as it spun on an imaginary axis and rounded the curve in a perfect turn. "Good job, boys. Now there ain't but about a hundred of them between here and where we're goin'," Gus commended his crew.

The two rafts following negotiated the turn as well, and the raftsmen enjoyed open water for awhile. A short time later, the Lumber City trestle came in sight. Gus knew this could be tricky, but if you got your heading right, the rest was easy.

"Got to steer a little more to the white side," Gus shouted.

"Gotcha," Bob responded heaving his oar to the right of the raft. This brought the bow about to the left.

These commands have an interesting origin. It seems that in times past, lands to the south and west of the river had been owned by Indians under treaty. Those on the north and east by white settlers. Hence the left side of the river, as one proceeded downstream, was known as the white side and the right side was known as the Injun side.

Gus eye-balled the alignment of his craft and estimated that he'd be able to pass under the trestle without any problem. "That's good. Steady as she goes." Now I hope that ferry ain't in the way, he thought.

The raft slipped under the trestle as neat as could be, clearing it by at least six feet on each side. The ferry was safe on the

Lumber City side.

Below Lumber City, the Ocmulgee and Oconee Rivers join to form the Altamaha at a junction known as "Helltown." Ordinarily the waters are fairly calm at this union, but the Oconee, which is fed by waters from the hills of North Georgia, sometimes causes a problem due to the larger volume of water. Raftsmen sometimes lose control of their craft and go into a spin, causing the raft to break apart or run aground.

Gus was well aware of this hazard, and prepared for it. Near the right side of the river, the waters eddied back up the river. Since the river was full, the risk of shallow water was small. Guiding the bow of the raft into the edge of the eddy, Gus moved cautiously out of the backing waters to the left. The faster waters from the Oconee caught the bow, pulling it into the main stream. The stern of the raft followed smoothly and the rough merging waters were negotiated.

The waters were a little rougher here, but they would soon smooth out. The speed of the current was faster now due to the larger volume in the narrower channel. The increased speed would make it possible to cover more distance. Gus hoped to be able to tie up at the mouth of a creek, near Town's ferry, for the night.

The winter night began to fall. It seemed to come more rapidly in the shade of the swamp. Spying his intended camp site, Gus and the crew guided the raft to a berth just above the mouth of the creek. This location had the advantage of a slower current for tying up and the added benefit of the creek current to accelerate the raft as they cast off in the morning.

Securing lines at the bow and stern to large trees on the bank, the raftsmen settled in to prepare for the night. The other two rafts had been secured upstream and the men joined to share their evening meal.

Rafting food was usually simple fare. Bacon, beans, and potatoes were staple foods for the crew. The foods were cooked, mostly fried, over an open fire in a frying pan. The men would often take turns cooking the meal. Sometimes, one man would be selected to cook. He usually received extra pay for this duty.

After supper, the crew sat and chatted by the warm fire. All sorts of tales were told at these fireside chats. The most popular were about ghosts and strange unexplained happenings. Other men talked about their dreams and the future.

Jack was particularly fond of ghost stories. He usually told at least one, given the chance.

"Boys, the strangest thing happen to me the other night. I was walkin' by the farm and I heard this noise, sounded like a baby crying. Well, sir, I thought there was a young'un lost off from its Ma. I begun to look for the baby, but I couldn't find nothin'. A few days later I was tellin' some folks about my experience and they told me that a woman kilt her baby on that farm once upon a time. They say you can still hear the young'un crying ever now and then in them trees near the path. Honest."

Some of the men nodded in agreement. The belief in ghosts and goblins was rather widespread, so no one questioned Jack's experience. Gus didn't say anything, but he was skeptical of these stories and figured the sounds were a combination of the wind and Jack's overactive imagination.

Jack's tale led to other stories, some more bizarre than his.

The group fell silent and someone said, "Gus, you're awfully quiet. Ain't you got nothin' to say tonight?"

"I reckon not, I ain't much of a yarn spinner."

"Aw, you musta heard some tale or other."

"Well, I heard this tale about a school teacher one time."

"Tell us."

Gus decided to pour it on. "Well, it seems there was this feller by the name of Icky, or some such name. Anyhow, Icky taught school in one of them country schools away up the country. He was a powerful mean cuss, and didn't hardly nobody like him.

"It seems that Icky and this other feller was sweet on the same gal. Miss Prunelli, or somethin' like that.

"Well, this feller decided he'd get rid of Icky, so he dressed up in these black clothes and made hisself up like he didn't have no head. Then as Icky was a comin' back from courtin' Miss

Prunelli, this headless horseman come on him in the woods. It looked like the feller had his head under his arm as he rode toward Icky. Just as he got close to Icky, he throwed his head at Icky.

"Well, to make a long story short, Icky got the hell out of there and didn't come back."

"Where'd you hear that?"

"Ma read it in a book one time."

"You don't say."

"Yeah, there's fun things in books, too. Maybe you ought to learn to read yourself."

The men began to yawn and stretch. "I understand this same fellow wrote a story about a guy who went to sleep and slept for twenty years," Gus added.

"That's somethin' I could do," Bob concluded. The raftsmen left for their respective craft and turned in for the night.

Gus lay in his bedroll listening to the sounds of the night. If there were a more peaceful place on earth, he didn't know where you would find it. He drifted off to sleep with the music of nature singing in his ears.

* * *

The winter dawn arrived, accompanied by a heavy fog. The waters of the river were considerably warmer than the air. Consequently, the fog rose from the river, blanketing the surrounding area.

Gus arose and stoked the fire. "Time to rise and shine, boys," he called.

Bob rolled over in his bedroll, "I'm a risin', but I'll be damned if I'll shine."

"I don't really care if you shine or not. Just get your butt out of the sack. There's work to be done," Gus responded.

Groaning his displeasure, Bob rolled out and stowed his bedroll in the tepee. Jack was up and about now. The day's chores were underway.

The raftsmen cast off from their night mooring and proceeded down river. Shortly, they passed Town's Ferry and continued through some of the most difficult water on the Altamaha, places where the river ran straight for a long stretch and then narrowed at a point would sometimes create a whirlpool known as a "suck." Rafts were known to break apart under the strain of these whirlpools.

They were now approaching such a point. Gus studied the current for some time before he made his judgement.

"Boys, I think we'll head to the Injun side and see if we can get her goin' fast enough to get the bow over. If we can do that, we'll be okay. This stick pile's put together right well, if I do say so myself. We need all the speed we can get, so hump them oars."

"Gotcha," Bob and Jack replied.

The raft gained speed as the men lay to on the oars. By pulling to the side, they were able to use the natural force of the water to assist them as they navigated the whirlpool. The bow passed into the swirl and the front of the raft started to spin. Gus, on the bow oar, held his sweep steady and the bow corrected and came out over the suck. The logs on the raft bucked like a wild horse as they rolled across the whirlpool, but they didn't break apart.

Gus tried to compensate for the energy of the whirlpool by letting the raft swing wide on the point. He misjudged the force of the current and the raft grounded on the bank.

It wasn't the best of times to call someone to his aid, but he needed help. "Bob, get up here and give me a hand. Jack, stay on the stern. Try and hold'er, if you can."

Bob sprang into action, mostly because he was frightened out of his wits. Gus thought, that's the fastest he's moved the whole trip.

The two men were able to push the raft clear of the bank. As the bow released, the stern swung about and the craft floated free.

Gus inspected the raft as the journey continued. All the joints had held, but he didn't think it would be safe to leave them as they were. Approaching Jack, who was on the stern oar, Gus said, "I'll relieve you here awhile. The raft needs tightening. How about takin' a mall and makin' sure there are no loose joints? Then take a turn or two on them rope binders."

Looking back, Gus could see that the other two rafts were following along, having negotiated the suck as well or better than his own craft. "Boys, check your joints. We've got more of these waters ahead," he called.

The remaining hours of the day went well and they made it past Nail's Ferry, Mann's Ferry and below Piney Bluff to a place called Dead River. Here, Gus decided to camp for the night.

Raftsmen did all kinds of things to amuse themselves and to help with their survival. One of these was fishing. Jack was an avid fisherman. His custom was to tie a line to the raft and let it trail in the water. This trolling would sometimes produce a nice fish which gave the raftsmen some variety in their diets. So far, what with the high water and sometimes rough steering, he had not caught any fish. He decided to bait his hook and set it out tonight. Cutting a piece of bacon from their side meat, Jack placed it over the side of the raft.

Early the next morning while everyone was asleep, Gus was awakened by a sound of splashing water. At first, he wasn't quite sure what was happening, then he remembered Jack's fishing line. Sure enough, there on the river side of the raft, the water was boiling and the set line was singing through the inky water.

"Jack, wake up! I think you've caught a whale."

Jack rolled out of his bedroll and scrambled to his set line. He reached for the line to haul in his catch. It was a good thing the line was securely fastened to the raft because it was immediately jerked from his grasp. "Gus, I'm gonna need some help with this one!"

Gus watched the line move a bit. "I think you best let him tire himself out a while."

The fish continued to fight the line for some twenty minutes, then he left off fighting and simply lay still in the water. By now, daylight had dawned and the men from the other rafts were in on the excitement.

It is not uncommon to catch catfish weighing as much as forty pounds in the Altamaha River. This one wasn't a record, but Gus guessed that he weighed twenty pounds. This would certainly be a welcome change from bacon and beans at every meal.

Gus helped Jack haul the fish aboard the raft. It was a matter of a few minutes to dress him and soon the smell of fresh frying fish floated over the river, enticing everyone within nose-shot. The men breakfasted on fresh catfish and sourdough hush-puppies. When everybody had his fill, the leftovers were stored for the rest of the trip.

Loosing their rafts, the journey continued. There were a few places that presented a challenge now, but the worst of the trip was behind. For the most part, the work now slowed to a snail's pace.

Down river, the sound of a steamboat whistle told them they were not alone on the river. Sound carries far over the water. Some raftsmen claim they could hear one another talking as much as forty miles apart at night, which was probably a tall tale. But the sound gave them plenty of time to prepare to meet the steamboat.

Gus ordered his crews to pull out of the channel. The progress of the rafts would be slower but he knew the steamboat would hog the channel. After some time, the sound of the paddle wheels could be heard churning the red muddy waters of the river. The boat came in sight and slowly made its way upstream.

She was a stern wheeler. During the 1800s, side wheelers had been experimented with on the Altamaha, but the experience wasn't good because of the narrow channel in some parts of the river. Steamboats had made regular runs as far as Macon on the Ocmulgee and Milledgeville on the Oconee, but they were not as frequent since the railroads came to the area.

Gus and his men watched as the steamboat churned by like a giant foaming at the mouth, backing up the river. The sight never failed to make an impression on Gus. He often thought it would have been nice to pilot one of those monsters.

The raft proceeded past Stafford's Ferry, where a bridge would be built about a decade later, called Lane's Bridge. Then down river to Sister's Bluff, and on by Oglethorpe's Bluff, where legend had it, James Edward Oglethorpe, the founder of the Georgia colony, had escaped an Indian party by jumping his horse into the river. Night of the third day brought them within a short distance of Doctor Town.

Berthing the raft for the night, the men prepared their evening fare and made ready for the next day. Gus didn't run at night unless there was no way to avoid it. It was just too risky.

The weather had been good so far this trip. Gus knew that it was unlikely to continue. And sure enough, it didn't. The cold winds began to blow from the northwest, and rain soon accompanied them. The men huddled in their tepee to keep dry. The fire spit and sputtered as the raindrops steamed away before the fury of the fire. Fortunately, the tepee was well constructed and withstood the winds.

The rains had slacked somewhat by morning. The raftsmen decided to castoff and head down stream. The overcast sky still threatened to drench them, but the heavy rains did not come. They actually saw the sun a couple of times that day.

On the fifth day, the raftsmen made their way into Darien. This seacoast town had been, and still was, a thriving seaport. Ships from all over the world docked here to load their holds with cotton, timber, and other precious cargo for consumption in the Northern United States, Europe, and other parts of the world.

Several sawmills processed the timber floated down the Ocmulgee, Oconee, and Altamaha River system. The timber market was usually better here than at other points on the river simply because the demand for good timber was higher.

Gus and his crew delivered their rafts to the sawmill that had been designated to receive their timber. In this case, payment would be mailed to the timber seller, so the paper work consisted of obtaining a receipt showing that the merchandise had been transferred.

Their business completed, the men went into town for a bit of rest and relaxation before beginning their return trip. Gus had been authorized to draw a bank draft to pay wages at the end of the trip. He now dispensed the allotted pay to each crew member.

"Okay, boys, this is it. This is what you've got comin'. If you're a mind to blow it in town, that's your headache," he said, as he completed the payroll.

One of the top priorities after several days on a raft was a bath and shave. Everybody smelled of wood smoke and grime accumulated as a result of several days of going without washing. One might wonder why, with all the river water available, these men didn't bathe more often. First, it was winter and there simply were not the conveniences needed to warm water and bathe the body. Secondly, there was no way to wash and change clothes. Consequently, the raftsmen were in a rather grimy condition upon the completion of a trip.

Boarding houses usually served the raftsmen with the needed amenities to tidy up. Here one could not only rent a room, but all the other comforts they ordinarily wanted.

After their baths, the men were disposed to go looking for entertainment. There were plenty of places where you could buy whiskey, or anything else you desired, including feminine companionship. Many of the men were married, but that didn't keep them from philandering.

Gus joined the rest of the crew at a local watering hole. He ordered himself a drink and surveyed the women who were on hand to entertain the customers.

"Howdy, handsome," a floozy blond said, as she sidled up to Gus's seat. "Want some company?"

In times past, Gus would have accepted the invitation, but now he had other priorities. "No, thanks."

"What's the matter? Ain't good enough for you?"

Gus looked her squarely in the face and replied, "It's not you. I've just got other things on my mind."

The blond grinned knowingly, "Got a girl back home, huh?"

Gus finished his drink and set the glass on the bar. "Yeah, something like that. Here, buy yourself a drink," he said, slipping a four bit piece in her hand.

"Thanks, handsome," the blond said, as Gus walked out the door.

Gus found the jewelry store down the street. As he walked in the door, an elderly gentleman met him and asked, "Something I can do for you, young man?"

"I'd like to price a ring."

"We have several. What price range did you have in mind?"

"Just something nice, but not too expensive."

"Let me show you what we have."

The crew spent the night in Darien. The next day, they left for Brunswick by steamboat. They would catch the train there and return to Lumber City.

Gus would make many more trips between now and the close of the logging season. As he considered his experiences on this trip, he thought, I wonder which part of the river is wilder, the natural part or the town at the end of it?

Chapter 7
The Proposal

Spring arrived and the world began to turn its many shades of green as the new growth appeared. The river swamp was gloriously beautiful with its covering of poplar, bay and other magnificent trees and flowering plants. Animals began their annual spring mating rituals. The world had awakened to a fresh start and a new cycle of life.

Eva felt new and refreshed after a long winter of dreary bare trees and flowerless plants. Spring was her favorite season. She took advantage of all the time she could to tend her flowers and simply enjoy the outdoors. Flowers were blooming in her flower garden, and the world was as beautiful as she could remember.

There was just one major flaw. She had not seen enough of Gus. He came by occasionally on his way back to camp from delivering a raft of timber to market, but it seemed these visits were too few and far between. Right now, she was dreaming that he would show up and carry her far away. There they would live happily ever after. She knew in her mind that this was a fairy tale, but a girl could dream, couldn't she?

She had looked down the lane for the umpteenth time this morning to see if Gus was coming. Each time was just as disappointing as the one before. She might as well give up and turn her attention to something more useful. Hang that man anyhow, she thought.

Noon came and went, and the day's chores had to go on. It didn't matter what happened in the rest of the world, on the farm, the work must be done. Eva had reconciled herself to the fact that Gus wasn't coming today when she heard a hail at the front gate.

"Hello, anybody home?" a strong, male voice called.

Eva stood and pulled back the sitting room curtain where she had been mending some clothes. Gus was standing at the gate as big as life. She wanted to rush out and greet him, but she decided she would be a bit cool. Restraining herself as best she could, she called, "Estell there's somebody at the gate. Would you see who it is?"

Estell, who was coming from the kitchen answered, "Okay," as she came down the hall to the front door. Opening the door, she saw Gus waiting patiently at the gate.

"Why, it's Gus Reynolds. Come on in, Gus."

"Thanks, Estell. Is Eva home? I'd like to see her if I could."

"I think she's here somewhere," Estell said, going along with Eva's ploy.

"You come on in and wait in the sittin' room while I see if I can find her."

Gus followed Estell into the hallway and then into the sitting room on the right. "If you'll have a seat, I'll go get her."

Estell found Eva in the kitchen. "What are you doin'? You've been watchin' the road all day for him, and now you send me out to meet him."

"That's just the reason. I don't want him to think I'm anxious to see him."

Estell looked disgusted, "If a man went to as much trouble to court me as he does you, I'd certainly be nicer to him."

"Oh, well, you can be sure I ain't gonna let him get away, but I don't think it's good for him to know how eager I am to see him."

"Suit yourself," Estell said, leaving the kitchen by way of the back door.

Eva sauntered to the sitting room and walked in as casually as she could. "Why, ain't this a pleasant surprise," she said, seating herself in a chair opposite Gus.

Gus grinned a bit self-consciously and said, "I hoped it would be."

"What in the world are you up to today?" Eva inquired

conversationally.

"To tell you the truth, I came to see a certain young lady because I've got something I want to talk over with her."

"You don't say. Well, what is it you wanted to talk about?"

Gus shifted in his seat, "It's kind of personal."

"Oh, well, what was it?"

Gus thought he could detect a tremor in her voice and a gleam in her eye. I've got this one figured, he thought.

"Why don't we go for a walk and discuss it?"

Eva consented by rising from her chair and preceding Gus down the hallway into the front yard and down the lane. They found themselves near the entrance of the lane where a tree stump had been left for a seat to be used while waiting near the road for a ride. They seated themselves side by side.

"As you know, I've made quite a few trips to Darien this past winter," Gus said.

"Yes, what about them?"

"Well, I found this while I was there, and I thought I'd see if you'd like to wear it for me."

Darn this man anyhow, Eva thought, he never comes directly to the point and he knows my weakness for trinkets. Aloud she said, "It depends on what you're askin' me to wear."

Gus handed her a small package wrapped in fine paper tied with ribbon. With heart beating wildly, but trying not to show it, Eva opened the packet and gazed at the rings nestled in the box. She managed not to gasp as she said, "It's beautiful. This is a wedding set, isn't it?"

Gus slipped to his knees, he felt silly doing it, but here goes, he thought. "Miss Eva Hester," he said, as solemnly as he could muster, "would you marry me?"

This was just the sort of thing Eva had dreamed of, but she decided to be cautious. "I'm not sure. You'll have to talk to Pa."

"I'll do that."

Eva smiled, "If it's okay with him, I'll marry you."

Gus rose from his knees with a shout, "Yahoo."

Reaching down, he swept Eva into his arms. Holding her as

close as he could, he kissed her full on the lips, savoring their sweetness. Eva kissed him back as fiercely as she could.

For a long time, Gus held her, then released her and stood back to admire her again. This young woman never failed to enchant him with her impish smile and sparkling eyes. She was a joy to be with. He thought he would love her as long as he lived.

The euphoria of the moment passed, but the glow of the encounter lasted for some time. Gus was determined to conclude his business with Eva's father as soon as possible. With this in mind, he stayed until he could have an opportunity to talk with him.

Eva had suggested that she talk to her father first. She found him at the barn repairing a piece of harness. Bill Hester was usually a patient man, and he always found time to talk to Eva. Besides, she had a way of persuading him to hear her out on almost any subject.

"Pa, I need to talk to you."

"What's it about?"

"You know I've been seeing Gus for some time now."

"Yes, I sort of noticed that."

"Pa, he's got something to talk to you about."

"He has, has he? What?"

"I'll let him tell you, but it involves my future happiness."

"Oh, I see. Well, send him on around."

Eva left, and soon Gus entered the barn where Bill was seated working at his bench. "Uh, Mr Hester?"

"It's okay, boy, go on. I ain't gonna bite your head off."

"Well, sir, as you know, I've been seein' Eva for awhile now."

"Yes, we were just remarkin' on that."

"I've gotten to be real fond of her. As a matter of fact, I'm in love with her."

"You sure about that, son?"

"Yes, sir, as sure as I've ever been of anything in my life."

"Well, what you got in mind?"

Gus shifted from on foot to the other, "I want to marry her."

"I see. Well, now, I can't say this comes as a surprise. Marriage is a serious step," Bill said, as he laid his work aside and faced Gus.

"Yes, sir, I know."

Bill looked at Gus for a minute, then said, "How do you plan to support her?"

Gus changed feet, "I've been savin' for some time now, and I've accumulated some money. My Pa'll let me have some land to build a house, and I've always been a hard worker. I think we'll make it just fine."

"Sounds like you've thought this thing out right well."

Gus smiled nervously, "Thank you, sir."

Bill looked thoughtful for a bit, "I think Eva's in love with you, boy. She's been showin' all the signs lately. I'm goin' to give my consent under one condition."

"What's that, sir?"

"You be good to her. If you can't live with her, admit it, and don't go being mean to her. You get my meanin'?"

"Yes, sir."

"If that's understood, I'd be happy to have you in the family."

Gus left the barn walking on air. He had never been more happy in his entire life. There were a thousand things he wanted to do. He felt like telling the whole world he was in love.

The evening meal gave an opportunity to announce the engagement. Gus and Eva were seated next to each other at the table. Bill spoke, "Let me have your attention everybody. Before we have the blessing, Gus and Eva have an announcement to make."

Gus hesitated. Eva didn't say anything either.

"Well, cat got your tongue?" Bill teased.

Gus held up Eva's left hand. The new ring sparkled in the lamp light. The other girls sighed. Eva blushed. Gus finally found his voice. "Eva and I are goin' to be married."

"When?" a chorus of voices asked.

"We've still got to pick the date, but it won't be long," Gus answered.

During the meal the whole family was abuzz with questions. Most of the queries went unanswered simply because there was no answer. The girls wanted to know if they could get new dresses for the occasion. The boys wanted to know if there would be a wedding celebration. Gus and Eva decided they would like to be alone. Alas, it was not to be.

After supper, the family gathered in the sitting room. Bill got out his banjo and played. Gus was expected to dance with all the girls. He thought he would never get back to Eva.

Estell and Eva went back to the kitchen to fetch something to drink. Estell had been dying to get Eva alone for hours now. This was the best chance she would have.

"I'm so happy for you, Sis. This is wonderful."

"Thank you. I'm glad you approve."

"Gus is really nice. I hope you'll be very happy."

Eva looked at her sister thoughtfully, "Everything's happened so fast. I don't know if I'm ready for all this."

"Sure you are, Sis. You'll make it just fine."

"I don't know. There are a million things to do."

Estell hugged her, "I'll help you with everything. Don't worry."

"I really appreciate that," Eva said, as they returned to the sitting room carrying the drinks.

The celebration lasted well into the night. Everyone was tired, and the family was a bit late getting started the next morning. Gus had stayed overnight and was planning to return home today.

He and Eva finally found time to talk before he departed.

"I have to go home now, Eva. My folks need me, and there's a ton of work to be done."

"I know, I'm overwhelmed by everything myself."

Gus reached for her hands. Placing them in his, he said, "I'll work hard, and we'll get ready for the weddin' as soon as possible. I want us to have a proper place to live when we get married."

"What're your plans?"

"I'm goin' to ask Pa for that piece of land down near that

little creek on our place. Then I'll get the proper materials and we'll build us a house."

"How long do you figure that'll take?"

"I'm not sure, but if all goes well, we ought to be able to have the lumber by fall. We could get married soon after we get the house built."

"That'd be good. It'll give me plenty of time to prepare for our weddin'."

Gus grinned, "I can't hardly wait. What I'd really like to do is whisk you off to the justice of the peace and get married right away."

"I know, me too, but my folks would never forgive me."

Gus sighed, "I'd feel like a heel not havin' a proper home to take you to. It just wouldn't work."

Eva was glad he had a practical side to him. If not, she would be tempted to give in and go with him on impulse. She decided it was good to have a stable man.

Gus held her and kissed her. Releasing her, he said, "I'd better be on my way. I'll see you next weekend."

Eva watched him go quietly, resisting the urge to hold him one more time. After all, she knew this man had a love of the great outdoors, and this wasn't the last time she would have to watch him walk away.

Chapter 8
House Raising

Summer came, and with it all the heat and hard work so familiar to South Georgians. The fields were producing weeds abundantly and the turpentine boxes had to be worked. It was difficult to put anything else into an already busy schedule, but Gus had declared that he would make the time.

He approached Alonzo about the land and house for Eva and himself. "Pa, I'd like to talk to you."

Alonzo, who was reading a week-old newspaper, looked up. "What's it about, Son?"

"I've asked Eva to marry me."

"I'm not surprised. What was her answer?"

"She said 'yes.'"

"Well, congratulations."

"Thanks."

"What now, Son?"

Gus seated himself across from Alonzo. "We'll be needin' a place to live."

"Have you thought this out?" Alonzo said, as he lay aside his newspaper.

"Yes, I have, Pa."

"Well, how can I help you?"

Gus measured his words carefully. He didn't want to appear to be selfish. "I was hopin' I could have a small piece of land to build us a house on."

"Where'd you have in mind?"

"I kind of fancy that spot down by the creek near where the road forks."

"Oh, the one with the nice water oak?" Alonzo asked as he shifted in his seat.

"That's the one."

"I see. What about building materials?"

Gus leaned back in his chair and crossed his legs. "I've saved most of my wages from workin' the loggin' camps the past winter. I can buy windows and such with that. I thought we might cut some trees off your place for the lumber."

"Who's goin' to mill it for you?"

"I thought I'd ask Uncle Homer. He's got that portable steam job. We could set it up not far from the house, and we wouldn't need to haul the lumber too far."

"That sounds like a good plan. I think it'd work out just fine. If I could afford it, I'd buy one of them small mills. But you know what they say, 'If wishes was horses, beggars would ride.'"

"Thank you, Pa. I'll get started on it right away."

Gus went to see Homer, and he agreed to let him use the sawmill. The next step was to select the timber.

There was still virgin timber on the Reynolds' farm. Tall round stands of beautiful pine trees that could be sawed so that a knot was rarely seen in a board. Gus went through these trees selecting those he felt would give him the best and most lumber for his labor. He carefully marked each tree so that he would be able to find it when he returned to cut the timber.

He was also careful not to clear cut any area in the woods. Clear cutting was a poor practice, because it didn't allow for cover for new growth, and it also destroyed natural habitat for wildlife. Hunting was a prized activity by farmers. It wasn't a sport as moderns see it; it was a means of survival.

Harvesting the timber was perhaps the most challenging part of the process. The trees were felled with a crosscut saw, topped with an axe, sawed into the required lengths, and dragged to the desired location. The logs were then allowed to season, dry out, before they were cut into boards.

Gus picked a mill site across the creek from his building location. This would keep the amount of debris down near his house, but would not be too far to move the sawed lumber. Alonzo had also considered this spot as a possible location for a more permanent mill.

Homer had agreed to loan Gus the mill and also agreed to deliver and set it up. He arrived about mid-morning. Gus was at the log brow when the team pulling the steam engine approached.

The driver hitched the reins over the brake handle of the wagon and dismounted. "Where you gonna set this rig up?"

"Just run it over there where the land starts to fall away toward the creek. That way we can pull the sawdust down hill."

"Okay, sounds good to me."

Gus watched as the driver led the team to the place he had indicated. "I think she needs to go ahead a little more. We need to get the platform and saw in behind here," Gus said, waving his hand to indicate the location.

The steam engine consisted of a boiler, engine proper, and pulleys to attach belts to drive the saw. This entire assembly was mounted on a set of metal wheels. It looked as if it were the leftover parts of a seventy-five year old locomotive.

A large belt would cover the drive pulley, then go around a pulley attached to the saw. Once the set-up was complete, the whole system would work rather smoothly.

Homer, himself, was driving the wagon carrying the saw platform assembly. It was the work of about half a day to set up the mill.

Gus wiped the sweat from his forehead, "I'm glad that's done."

"Yeah, me too," Homer seconded.

"Now I've got to get all this stuff sawed."

"You'll be needing some help, I reckon."

"Me and Sam can do most of it, but I could use one or two hands to help with the slab and board totin'."

Homer spat a stream of tobacco juice on the ground. "I could let a couple of my hands help, if you're amind."

Gus pulled the stopper from a water jug, took a swig, and slapped the stopper back in place. "I'll just let you know."

"Okay, don't get too big of a head of steam on that boiler or she'll blow sure as hell's hot," Homer said, as he mounted a mule of the team he had driven.

Homer and his hired hand rode off, leaving Gus to his work.

* * *

Sawing timber, even on a small scale, is hard work. First, the logs have to be loaded on the carriage. Gus had tried to make this easier by piling the logs so that they could be rolled onto the carriage with a cant-hook directly from the brow. This would work well for awhile, but eventually the logs would have to be dragged to the loading area.

The second step in the process is to saw the logs into the required sizes. The sawyer, the person who operates the saw, has to know how to rotate the log, what sizes; 2x4, 4x4, and so on, can best be cut from a given log. This takes a great deal of practice and can be done fairly easily by an experienced sawyer. Occasionally though, even the expert has to stop and make measurements that will help avoid waste.

The third step is really two-in-one. The saw dust is carried off by a drag chain attached to a post. Eventually the dust will form a pile. Some of these piles reach several feet in height depending on the length of time the mill is used in a particular location. While the operation is being done mechanically, the slabs, bark-sided cuts, are piled in one place to be used as fuel for the steam engine. At the same time, the boards of varying sizes are piled in drying stacks according to their size.

The job is at least a three-man operation. One man spots the log, that is, brings it to the carriage. This man also fires the furnace and assists in other ways. The sawyer cuts the lumber and maintains the saw, sharpens it, and so on. The slabber carries away the slabs and lumber. Sometimes teams of men work together on one job. When any worker has slack time, he is expected to help catch up in other areas.

Gus worked at this operation regularly. One or two of his brothers would assist him when they could take time off from the farm work. Occasionally, Gus would hire a hand for a day or two.

On more than one occasion, Gus would swap work with someone in order to get help with his task.

Persistence is the name of the game in any such endeavor. A typical day would begin at sunrise. The crew would work until mid-morning, take a break, and continue until noon. At mid-day they ate a meal, usually brought from home. Then, after a short rest period, any necessary maintenance would be performed. The work continued, with short breaks, until the sun began to hide its face in the western sky.

Gus disengaged the saw pulley as Sam carried the last 2 by 4 to its pile. "Let's break for noon."

"That sounds like a winner to me," Sam said, seating himself on a log.

Gus retrieved their dinner buckets and joined Sam on the log. They ate their meal without ceremony, chatting as they consumed the left-over breakfast foods Susie had packed.

Gus took a bite out of a biscuit and chewed it thoughtfully. "I think we're about through with the framing."

"That don't mean we're half through with the sawin', does it?" Sam asked.

"Nope, we've got to make lots more cuts for the weather boarding and floor. We've already got some of it, but it ain't near enough, by my reckonin'."

"How long you figure it'll take to finish the lumber?"

"Hard to tell. If we don't have a breakdown, I'd say maybe two more weeks."

Sam took a swig of water in between bites. "I'll be glad when this job's done."

Gus brushed biscuit crumbs off his hands. "You're not the only one. Pass me that water will ya?"

Gus poured a cup of water from the jug, lifted it to his mouth, and drained it in one draught. "The next job is to get the lumber to the building site."

Sam crunched a strip of bacon. "How long you figure before you'll start buildin'?"

"I'm hopin' to make a start in the fall. Maybe October."

"That'd be good. The weather'll be cooler an' the harvest'll be done."

"Yeah, that's what I'm countin' on."

The brothers finished their meal and lay back to rest. After about fifteen minutes, Gus sat up, pushed his hat back, and said, "Well, I reckon we'd better get a move on. This ain't buying the baby no hippies."

Reluctantly, Sam rose. "You're right. Let's go."

Gus and Sam were working short-handed today. In spite of this, they were able to accomplish a good deal. It had been Gus's experience that two men could sometimes do as much as three simply because there was less talking and carrying on between them.

The lumber piles were beginning to look impressive. Gus checked his estimated materials against the inventory again, just to make sure he had enough lumber to do the job. He usually allowed 10% or so for error. Everything was checking out fine.

That evening, Gus discussed his progress with Alonzo. "Pa, I been thinkin' I'd ought to go ahead and order the windows for the house."

Alonzo leaned back in his chair, stretched himself, and let out a sigh. "I think that might be a good idea. It takes awhile to get them sometimes."

Gus ran a toothpick between his teeth, clamped it firmly in his mouth, and put his hands together. "How 'bout I borrow old Doc and the one horse wagon to go to town tomorrow?"

"I don't see why not."

* * *

Next morning Gus, accompanied by Sam, hitched Doc to the wagon and made his way to Baxley. The local hardware on Comas Street either carried building supplies or would order them. Gus decided to stop here first.

"Can I help you?" a clerk greeted Gus as he walked through the door.

"I'm buildin' a house and thought I'd see what size windows

you had on hand."

"What size did you have in mind?"

"About 36 by 54 inches would do."

"Hm, let's see," said the clerk, looking at his ledger. "That's a popular size. I'm not sure we have 'em on hand. When did you need 'em?"

"Oh, about October."

"Good, that'll give us plenty of time to order 'em. How many you need?"

"I think six will be enough. I'll just put shutters over the others for awhile if I need to."

"Okay, I'll put in the order right away, and we'll let you know when they come in. Is there anything else?"

"Yeah, I need some nails."

"How many?"

"I'll start with a keg of 12s."

"Anything else?"

"Do you have brick? I'll need some for my chimneys."

"We'll need to order them."

"Okay, only I ain't sure how many I need."

"How about, I order 5000? If that's too many I'll always be able to sell 'em."

"Sure."

"What else?"

"I think that'll do it for now. You need a deposit?"

"Na, you can pay when you pick up the goods."

"Thanks."

"You're very welcome," the clerk answered as Gus exited the store.

Gus found Sam down the street at the B&B Café. "I'm finished with my store business. You got anything to do before we head back?"

"Not particularly. Just thought we might have a cup of java before we hit the road."

"Sounds good," Gus said, seating himself across the table.

The brothers picked up the keg of nails and returned home.

The day was well spent, so Gus decided not to do any mill work. There were other chores that needed his attention.

* * *

Meanwhile, Eva had an interest in the construction of the house, more exactly, decorating it. On one of Gus's frequent visits, she had asked him to give her some idea about the plans. Gus had drawn a floor plan with as much detail as he could. It was not an architect's work by any means, but it served the purpose.

Armed with the drawing, Eva began to make curtains for windows and plan for bedding clothes and the dozens of other little items that make a house a home, not just a shack to keep the weather out.

On one occasion, she and Gus made a trip to Hazlehurst to shop for fabrics. Actually, Gus wasn't really sold on the idea of being in a fabric shop, but he consented, to please Eva.

"How do you like this for sittin' room window curtains?" Eva asked.

"It sure has plenty of flowers."

"I like flowers."

Gus really wasn't too particular, "I think it would look nice."

"What about this for a table cloth?"

"You'll be cleanin' it most of the time. Do you think it'll wash up easy?"

"I think it will."

"It's fine with me, then."

The exchange between Gus and Eva went this way for the most part. She made her choices, and he agreed because he thought this was her decision anyhow.

"Don't you think we ought to look at a stove and some furniture?" Gus asked, after they had been shopping for sometime.

"Okay, let's go," Eva consented.

They found some furnishings on display, but for the most part, they had to look at drawings in catalogs. Most stores were not equipped to carry large inventories of goods.

"Here's the stove selection in our catalog," the clerk said, shoving the book across the counter.

Eva turned the pages slowly, "I don't see anything that I really like."

"How about this one with the warmer on top?" the clerk coached her.

"I don't know. It looks a little too big to me."

"Well, I suppose that depends on how many folks you gonna cook for, don't it?"

Gus and Eva decided to postpone choosing the stove for now. Looking at furniture was a different story. Eva found a bed that enchanted her, right on the floor of the store. She could just see it dressed in bed clothes. It would be beautiful. Gus consented and they bought it on the spot.

"That'll be ten dollars."

Gus retrieved a bill from his billfold and handed it to the clerk. "Just hold it for us. We'll pick it up later."

There were a number of these shopping trips over the months before the house was to be completed. Each one yielded some treasure that delighted Eva.

* * *

Finally, the sawing was complete. Gus moved the lumber, a wagon load at a time. As he hauled the material, he inspected each piece for knots, curls, and other flaws. Any piece that didn't meet his specifications was left in a seconds pile. These would be used for other building projects on the farm.

October arrived and all was ready for the construction to begin. Eva had been excited for weeks now. Her family would attend the house raising. She was beside herself with nervous energy to spare.

"Pa, is everything ready to go?" she asked for the tenth time.

"Calm down, young lady. We'll be leavin' in a few minutes," Bill reassured her.

Bill inventoried his tools once more and called, "I'm ready. How 'bout the rest of you?"

"Comin', Pa," he heard from everybody except Annie. She simply nodded as she came through the front gate.

They mounted the wagon and began their journey. "Pa, did you get your banjo?" someone asked.

"Got it stowed under the seat for safe keepin'," Bill replied.

* * *

The Reynolds' farm was a buzz of activity. Neighbors from all over the community had come to help with the house raising. This type of activity was their way of saying they wished the young couple well. It was also an opportunity to give them a gift of love and have a good time partying at the same time. As Alonzo would say, "They could kill two birds with one stone."

The men would build the house while the ladies held a quilting bee for the bride-to-be. Later, the women would prepare the meal and everybody would party.

Gus had decided on an L-shaped form for the house. The main body of the building, consisting of the sitting room and bed rooms, would form the long side of the L, while the kitchen, separated by a narrow breezeway, would form the short side. A porch across the front, and another inside the L, would complete the house.

The first step in the construction of the house was laying the foundation. Foundation blocks of wood with a high tar content were chosen and placed to support the framing. The high tar content made them more rot-resistant. Next, the floor joists were laid over these. Care was always taken to be sure these were level. Now the framing was constructed in sections and mounted atop the floor joists. Finally, the rafters were put in place.

Gus asked men who would now be considered master carpenters to take charge. These men would supervise the construction of some portion of the building assisted by several helpers. The cutting and measuring had to be done precisely to avoid waste. The supervisor was responsible for most of this.

Meanwhile, the ladies had been at the house. Two quilting frames had been set up and they were taking turns stitching the tops together with a cotton batting between them. This activity was not only functional, but afforded them an opportunity to socialize and catch up on the latest gossip. The upcoming wedding was naturally a topic of immense interest.

"Eva, when's the weddin'?" asked Miss Addie.

"We've not picked a date yet. It'll probably be sometime in the spring. We feel like we ought to get everything ready before we get married."

"That sounds sensible to me. But, tell me, ain't you just a little anxious?"

Eva blushed slightly, "Yes'em."

Miss Addie reached for a spool of thread and re-threaded her needle. Using her teeth, she bit the thread in two and said, "Well, we all think Gus is a mighty fine young man. You're sure a lucky girl."

"Thank you, ma'am," Eva said, quietly.

Miss Addie looked at Susie, "You're gettin' a fine daughter, too, Susie."

"I agree," Susie answered.

The conversation varied widely during the course of the morning. When noon approached, Susie said, "Goodness, look at the time! We'd better get the food down to the house."

There wasn't a place under any roof that would have been big enough to feed all the workers. Some of the men had set up sawhorses and laid boards over them to form a table. Here the noon meal was spread. Each family had brought food and there was no lack of it. When the meal was spread, Susie got Alonzo's attention. He, in turn, called to the workers.

"Come on boys, let's eat."

The men paused in the middle of whatever they were doing and came to the table. "Lord, we thank you for these friends and family gathered here today. We thank you for this food and ask you to bless us as we receive it. Amen," Alonzo prayed.

Lines formed and everyone helped themselves to generous portions of food. The men seated themselves on lumber piles and any other thing raised high enough off the ground.

Homer found a place beside Gus, "Boy, that pile of boards is startin' to look like a house."

"Yeah, I was wondering if it'd ever get this far," Gus said, as he took a forkful of food.

"Sure it has, and it'll be finished before you know it."

"I'm thankful for all the help from my friends and family. It would be a long hard row without them."

"Heck, I'm just glad we can do it. You're overdue for this weddin'."

The meal over, the men took a short noon. Returning to their work, they attacked it with renewed vigor and the house fairly fell together. As the sun went down, the roof had been dried in and most of the weatherboarding was in place. The remaining work could be done by two or three men over a few weeks.

The women had been making preparation for the evening meal. Many of them used dishes they had especially fixed for the occasion. Noonday leftovers were also available. But the highlight of the meal was barbecued pork. Cap, short for Captain, had cooked a whole hog over flaming oak coals. The meat retained the smell and flavor of the wood, creating a culinary delight.

With a second sumptuous meal under their belts, everybody was ready to party, especially the younger ones. Most of the old folks sat and rested while the youth danced to the music of the banjo, fiddle, and guitar. If you think this strange, you've forgotten the resilience and vigor of youth.

Gus was thankful to be with Eva at last. As they danced to a waltz, he held her and said, "You're beautiful tonight."

Eva flashed him a smile, "Why, thank you."

"You know, I wouldn't mind if this night went on forever."

"That'd be an awful long night, wouldn't it?"

"Not with you in my arms."

"I'm glad."

Gus and Eva found a seat on a bench that had been rigged from timbers laid on pieces of log.

The stars were brilliant in the sky. Venus, the evening star, sparkled in the western sky as the harvest moon rose in the east casting a brilliant flood of light over the landscape.

Eva leaned her head on Gus's shoulder and asked, "Do you ever wonder how far away they are, the stars, I mean?"

Gus put his arm around her. "Sometimes. But right now I feel like I could reach up and touch one of them."

"I'd like that bright one there, the one in the west."

Gus reached up with his hand and laughed. "Well, I can't seem to get hold of it tonight, but that's no reason to quit reachin', is it?"

Eva smiled. "I hope not."

Chapter 9
The Wedding

There was still plenty of work to be done on the house. The finishing would take some time. The weather-boarding had to be finished. The interior had to be sealed, and there were hundreds of small tasks that had to be done. Furnishings had to be bought or made. Gus and Eva had finally decided to buy a stove. They had already purchased a bed and some other odds and ends. Gus would build the dining table and other pieces of furniture as he had need and opportunity.

Eva busied herself with wedding preparations. She wanted this day to be special. After all, a girl has a first, and hopefully, only wedding, once. She especially wanted a nice dress.

Due to an old superstition, the groom wasn't supposed to see the wedding dress. Eva had to get her dress material without Gus knowing what it was. To accomplish this, she asked George to accompany her to Hazlehurst to shop for dress materials and other things she wanted to buy for the wedding.

"Come on, Sis," George called. Then thought to himself, women, they're never ready on time.

"Hold your horses," Eva answered from the hallway, "I'll be along in a minute."

"There now, I'm ready," Eva declared as she bounded out of the front door, down the steps, and through the gate, her red hair bouncing merrily around her shoulders.

"It's about time," George said, as he offered her a hand up as she mounted the wagon.

George climbed aboard and slapped the reins. The horse broke into a trot down the lane. Eva looked at George with a slight bit of irritation. "What's the all-fired hurry?" she demanded.

"I just don't want to take all day. That's all."

"Why? What you up to?"

"It ain't none of your business."

"I'll bet it's that Moore girl, ain't it? You got a date with her?"

"Maybe," George said, as he slowed the horse to enter the road from the lane. The rest of the drive was completed in silence.

There were not many places in Hazlehurst to shop. Actually, there was only one millinery and dress shop in the town. Otherwise, the general stores were your only choice. George stopped the wagon in front of the dress shop. Eva dismounted and entered the store, saying over her shoulder, "I'll be about an hour. You can pick me up then." George didn't reply.

As Eva opened the door, she was greeted by a middle-aged lady with premature graying hair. "Hello, I'm Mrs. Pearl. How may I help you?"

"I'm looking for material for a dress. That is, a weddin' dress," Eva answered.

"We have several designs. Do you sew or will someone else be making the dress? We offer dress-making services, you know."

Eva spotted a counter with some fabric that looked attractive, "I'll be doing my own work, thank you."

"Let me show you what we have here. If you don't like anything, we have a catalog that we can order from."

Mrs. Pearl carefully sorted through the different kinds of cloth calling them by their knit patterns and colors. Most of this didn't mean much to Eva. She just wanted something that looked nice and wasn't too expensive. Finally, she made a selection.

"Why don't you check this in front of the mirror?" Mrs. Pearl suggested.

Eva walked across the store to the full length glass, a definite luxury for the times, and held the cloth across her body, checking the contrast of her face with the color of the fabric. She decided she wasn't quite satisfied with the result.

Returning to the table with the cloth in hand, she said, "Let me try another."

Mrs. Pearl selected a bolt and handed it to Eva. "I think this would look lovely on you."

Eva repeated the mirror routine, but rejected this choice, too.

"Here, how about this one?" Mrs. Pearl suggested.

Eva stood before the mirror longer this time. This seemed more to her liking. "This'll do just fine," she said, handing the bolt of cloth to Mrs. Pearl.

"That's a good choice. Will there be anything else? What about a pattern?"

Eva nodded and said, "Yes, I'll need a pattern."

Mrs. Pearl reached under the counter and pulled out a box of patterns. "Here, see if you like any of these?"

Eva looked at the sketches of half a dozen dresses, made a selection, placed the remaining packets back in the box, and handed the box back. "I was thinking I'd like to look at a hat."

"I have a beautiful one that matches your cloth," Mrs. Pearl said, as she crossed the store to the rack of hats.

Standing before the mirror, Eva tried on the hat. "Could I add a ribbon?" she inquired.

"Certainly, a ribbon would go nicely with it," Mrs. Pearl said, retreating across the room to fetch a ribbon.

Returning with the ribbon she asked, "How's this?"

Eva took the strip of cloth and fitted it over the hat, tying the ribbon under her chin. She turned first one way, then the other, checking her profile. Finally, she said, "This'll do just fine."

Mrs. Pearl took the dress fabric to a cutting table and clipped the required amount from the bolt of cloth. She then folded it neatly. Returning to the main counter, she added up the purchase. Eva paid for her purchase and returned her change to her purse.

"Thanks for shopping with us," Mrs. Pearl said, as she handed Eva the package. "If there's anything else you need, I'll be happy to help you."

"I appreciate that," Eva said, as she turned to exit the store.

George drove up in a cloud of dust a few minutes later and they were soon on their way back to the farm.

* * *

Annie owned a foot-pedal Singer sewing machine, a really prized possession. Eva made use of this modern appliance to make her dress, but there was still lots of work that had to be done by hand. She also required the assistance of someone to help with the fitting. Estell was her choice, and a willing helper.

"Stand still. How am I supposed to fit this thing with you fidgetin' like that?" Estell questioned.

"If you weren't so dadburn slow, I'd be able to stand still," Eva asserted.

"Well, don't blame me if this don't fit."

"Okay," Eva sighed, resigning herself to the fact that this was going to take longer than she had hoped.

Finally, Estell stood up, "Go take a look in the mirror."

Eva moved to a position in front of the dresser mirror and turned as she watched herself in the glass. The dress made a pleasant swirl as she rotated back and forth. "Take up the waist just a little on the left," she said, holding a small fold of cloth to show where she wanted the tuck taken.

"Okay, but if you gain a pound between now and the weddin', it ain't gonna look right," Estell said, as she pinned the cloth in the indicated place.

Eva eyed the result critically, "That's better."

Day-by-day the dress took shape. Eva would sometimes remove a tuck here or there, take out stitches that didn't meet with her approval, and analytically examine each detail. Eventually, she had finished it somewhat to her satisfaction.

Not only was the dress a major part of the preparation, Eva had to decide how much food would be needed for the wedding guests. There would, of course be plenty. But the cooking and storing needed to be done well ahead, but not too far because of possible spoilage. She finally decided that a barbecue would be appropriate for the occasion.

* * *

Meanwhile, Gus had completed the house as best he could.

The inside work had been done. Now he would build those pieces of furniture that he could. This was an economy measure.

Selecting some of the best boards from his mill work, he painstakingly planed them to a smooth finish. With these, he covered a frame of boards, constructing a table that would serve his family for years to come. Not only his children would eat food from it, but his grandchildren and great-grandchildren.

Gus decided he needed a woman's input, so he asked Susie to come help him make some decisions. She had consented, and on several occasions she went to the house with Gus.

"Ma, what do you think?" Gus asked as they entered the kitchen.

"Son, everything looks okay to me."

"Don't you see anything that you'd change?"

"Son, every woman has different ideas about how a kitchen should be arranged. I can't tell you what Eva would like."

"I know that, but I want it to be as ready as it can be when we move in."

"I really don't think I can be of any more help. If you want more advice, I think you should bring Eva here and let her make some more of the decisions."

"I thought about that, but I wanted it to be a surprise."

"Some surprises ain't that good. Why not just wait until you're married and let her do it then?"

Gus thought for a minute, then made a decision. "That'll have to do."

* * *

Gus had a fondness for nice clothes, but he didn't own anything that he considered fit for his wedding. So he decided to buy himself a suit. With this in mind, he went shopping in Baxley.

Again, there wasn't much choice of stores for a man to outfit himself. A local dry goods shop on Main Street was probably his best chance to find something.

"Good afternoon. May I help you?" the clerk asked as Gus walked into the store with the sound of the door bell tinkling in his ears.

"Yeah, I'm looking to buy a suit of clothes."

"What did you have in mind?"

"Something dressy, probably in black or gray."

"Come with me."

Gus followed the clerk to the rear of the shop where a rack of men's suits hung. The clerk pulled a gray one from the rack and laid it across the other suits on the rack so that Gus could inspect it. Gus examined the fabric, inspected the seams, and checked the cut of the pockets. Removing the coat, he slipped it on and checked the fit. The shoulders were a bit narrow.

Gus stood better than six feet tall and had a slender build with broad shoulders. Ready-made clothes seldom fit without alterations. Buying any clothing was something of a chore for him.

"Here, try this one," the clerk said, pulling a larger size from the rack.

The coat fit better, but Gus thought the shade of gray didn't match him. "I'd like to try something in black," he said, removing the coat.

The clerk found a black suit, "Here, how about this one?"

Gus slipped the coat on. The shoulders fit. He liked the black better.

"We can have any alterations done for you if you'd like."

Gus tried on the pants behind a curtain. The waist was too large. Returning to the clerk he said, "I like this suit, but the waist will have to be taken in."

"That's not a problem. I can have them ready tomorrow. Will there be anything else?" the clerk asked as he hung the suit back on its hanger.

"I'll need a shirt and tie."

"Let's see what we have."

The shirt fitting had the same problems as the suit coat. Finally, Gus chose a white shirt with detachable collar that fit very well. The tie was a black string. A new black Stetson hat completed his new wardrobe for the wedding.

"How much?" Gus asked, as the clerk finished adding the

column of figures on his sales pad. Shoving the pad over the counter, the clerk showed the total to Gus. Gus paid the indicated amount and picked up his purchases.

As Gus exited the store, he met Homer. "Well, how's the expectant bridegroom?" Homer inquired.

"Not too bad, I reckon."

"When's the big day?"

"We about decided on the first Sunday in April."

"That's not too far away. Is there anything I can help you with?"

Gus looked thoughtful for a minute. "If you don't mind, I'd like to borrow your buggy for the weddin'."

Homer grinned, "I think I can spare it for awhile. Where you figure on honeymooning?"

"I'm not sure we'll go anywhere yet, but I'd like to take my new bride off in style."

"I think that can be arranged. How's your Ma and Pa? I ain't seen them for a spell."

"Oh, they're fine. I think Ma's just about as excited about this weddin' as me and Eva."

Homer pushed his hat back and scratched his head. "I reckon she is. It ain't every day your young'un gets married."

* * *

Gus spent most of the winter working on the house, so he had not made a raft trip this season. Now, with the house as complete as he could make it, and the wedding plans set he went to the swamps to work for awhile before the wedding. He needed the money to start life with Eva in a little better style.

Homer had decided to ship another raft or two of timber, so he hired Gus and a crew to deliver them. Gus worked up until the week before the wedding. He would return to the river again after they were married. After all, he would have a wife to provide for.

* * *

The Reynolds' household was in a state of confusion as they made ready to attend the wedding. Susie had prepared food to carry. She also had to make sure everything was just right for the children's clothes. They simply would not be seen sloppy for this occasion. Even Gus got more attention than he would have liked.

"Gus, you sure you got everything?" Susie asked for the tenth time.

"I'm sure, Ma."

"Be sure you have. It would embarrass me somethin' terrible if you left somethin'."

"Ma, I'm the one who's supposed to be nervous. It's my weddin', you know."

"I just can't help it, son. I want everything to be perfect."

Gus reached for her and gave her a hug. "It will be, Ma. Don't you worry."

Susie smiled nervously. "I'm proud of you, Son."

Gus looked her in the eye. "I'm proud of my Ma, and I'll do everything I can to keep her proud of me."

Finally, everything was ready. The family would take their own transportation, while Gus drove Homer's buggy. The trip would take the better part of a day, and they would have to stay overnight with the Hester's family.

Things were not calm at the Hester's home either. Eva was so excited she could hardly sit still to eat a meal. She checked a hundred times to see if she had missed anything. She inspected her dress for the umpteenth time to make sure she had not left anything undone. She was simply a bundle of nervous energy.

The arrival of Gus and his family added to the excitement. Everybody talked at once, and the whole place was abuzz with last minute preparations. Gus was grateful when he finally got Eva to himself for a minute.

"I'll be glad to get all this fuss over," he said, as they seated themselves on the settee.

Eva smiled nervously, "Me, too."

"Don't worry. Everything's gonna be all right," Gus said, putting his arm around her. She snuggled up to him and didn't say a word.

"Uh huh, now there'll be none of that," George teased, as he stepped through the sitting room door.

Gus took the teasing in stride, but Eva wasn't in the mood. "Go away, will you? Can't you see we're tryin' to talk?"

George sensed he was treading on dangerous ground. "I'll see you later," he said, as he exited the room.

Saturday night was spent with a sumptuous meal and dancing. The celebration had already begun and would continue until the couple were officially married. The men and boys took every opportunity to tease Gus. The ladies and girls did the same with Eva.

Estell got a chance to rib Gus while they were dancing. "You know that it's bad luck for the groom to see the bride on the weddin' day before they're married. So that means you can't see Eva in the mornin'."

Gus took the joke good naturedly. "Seems like I've heard that somewhere before. About a million times tonight."

"Well, I'm gonna make sure you don't see her just to be safe. I'm gonna hide her in her room until the ceremony."

The party wound down about midnight and everybody went to bed. The house was wall-to-wall bedding. Pallets where laid out all over the floor. The beds were reserved for the older folks. Some of the boys and young men elected to sleep in the hayloft in the barn. Eva was sure she couldn't remember when there had been this many people at their home overnight.

* * *

Sunday morning dawned. The sky was clear and the spring sun shown pleasantly on the yard. Birds added their song to the festivities of the day. Eva thought she had never seen a more perfect day.

"Estell, get up," Eva called as she turned over on the pallet in their room.

"What's the hurry? Gus ain't goin' nowhere."

"I know that, silly."

Estell was true to her word. This was the first time in a long time Eva could remember eating a meal in her room. She wasn't allowed out of her room until the ceremony.

Meanwhile, Gus was putting up with similar treatment. His brothers, especially, were riding herd on him. After awhile, he was able to make some preparations. He hitched the horse to the buggy and left the rig near the front of the house. When all the dirty chores were taken care of, he went to the house to get dressed. Susie had laid out his clothes for him. She was fussing over them when Gus got to the room.

"Gus, you get dressed now and call me when you're through."

"Ma, is that really necessary?"

"Just call me."

Susie left the room. Gus stripped himself and washed. Then he dressed in everything except his coat. He ran his comb through his hair as there was a knock at the door.

"Who's there?"

"It's your Ma."

"Okay, I'm decent. Come on in."

Susie slipped in the room closing the door behind her gently. She admired Gus in his new clothes. "My, ain't you a handsome young man?"

"Ma, I wish you'd let me be. I can get myself ready."

"I know that," Susie said, as she fussed with the collar of his shirt. She straightened it, then changed her mind and adjusted it again. "There now, that looks better."

Estell and Annie were helping Eva get dressed. Eva was so excited she could hardly stand still. "Quit squirmin'," Estell admonished her.

Eva looked down at her slip and pulled it to the left just a trace. She bit her tongue and didn't say anything.

Estell stood back and looked at Eva with a critical eye, "Ma, I think we're ready for the dress."

Estell and Annie lifted the dress over Eva's head and pulled it down into place. The full flowing cloth covered her, shining even in the dull light of the room. Her red hair, which had been brushed until it shown, contrasted with the hue of the cloth and her face glowed from the combination of the light and color.

Elder Thomas had arrived. Bill met him and invited him to sit in the sitting room. Gus was ushered in a few minutes later.

"So, young man, are you ready?" Elder Thomas asked.

"Yes, sir. Ready as I'll ever be."

"Don't worry, we hardly ever lose a bridegroom," he smiled.

"No, sir, I reckon not."

Elder Thomas leaned back in his chair. "Don't worry about a thing. Just follow my lead, and we'll get through this fine."

Bill came into the room, "Elder, I think we're ready to begin."

"That's good," Elder Thomas said, as he rose from his seat.

Everyone, except Eva and her father, gathered in the sitting room. The fiddler solemnly played, *Here Comes the Bride*, as Eva came into the room on Bill's arm. They stood before the minister as Gus joined them.

"Who gives this woman to be married to this man?"

"I do," Bill answered, as he stepped back and placed Eva's hand in Gus's.

"Dearly beloved, we are gathered here in the sight of God and this company to unite this man and this woman in holy matrimony. If anyone knows any cause that they should not be joined, let him speak now or forevermore hold his peace."

There was a pause and silence that seemed to last an eternity for Gus and Eva. Nobody made a sound.

"Hearing no objection, we will proceed with the wedding. Do you, William Augustus Reynolds, take this woman to be your lawful wedded wife, to love and to cherish, to honor and sustain her in sickness and in health, in poverty as in wealth, in the badness that may darken your days, in the good that may light your ways, and to be true to her till death do you part?"

"I do."

"Do you, Eva Victoria Hester, take this man to be your lawful wedded husband, to love and to cherish, to honor and obey him in sickness and in health, in poverty as in wealth, in the badness that may darken your days, in the good that may light your ways, and to be true to him till death do you part?"

"I do."

"Do you, Gus give a token of your love for Eva?"

Gus pulled the ring from his pocket and almost dropped it as he handed it to the minister.

"Place the ring on her left hand and repeat after me."

Gus slipped the ring on Eva's finger and looked at the minister.

"With this ring, I thee wed," intoned the minister.

"With this ring, I thee wed," echoed Gus.

"I pledge my love."

"I pledge my love."

"And with all my worldly goods I thee endow."

"And with all my worldly goods I thee endow."

"Gus and Eva, since you have consented, before God and these witnesses, to join in holy matrimony, by the power vested in me I now pronounce you man and wife. You may kiss the bride."

Gus and Eva faced each other, he placed his arms around her waist and kissed her full on the lips.

Elder Thomas said, "Ladies and gentleman, I present to you Mr. and Mrs. Reynolds."

The families rose from their seats. The once solemn assembly became a stir of celebration as the shouts of jubilation went up from both sides. The partying began.

There was plenty of food for everyone. It seemed to Gus that he had never seen so much food for the number of people. The music and dancing began and continued well into the afternoon.

Gus and Eva endured all the usual amenities, accepting congratulations here and there, acknowledging best wishes, and generally being whisked around by the tide of family and friends. At last, they felt they could exit gracefully.

Gus loaded Eva's trunk aboard the borrowed buggy and prepared to leave, but the couple had not gotten the last of their adulation from the crowd. As they made their way to the buggy, a throng met them with hands full of rice in celebration of an ancient fertility rite. The rice showered over them as they dashed for the buggy. Gus reached down, scooped Eva into his arms, and placed her on the buggy seat. Climbing aboard himself, he slapped the reins, and the horse started off down the lane with a spirited trot.

Everybody was shouting and waving. The younger boys chased the buggy as far as the end of the lane, ending their pursuit as they ran out of breath. Meanwhile, back at the house, the party continued.

Gus drove to Hazlehurst where he rented a room for the night at the small hotel. He could not afford to give Eva a honeymoon like he would have preferred, but he was determined that they would have some time together for awhile.

After checking in, the couple made their way to their room. Gus reached for Eva and held her as tightly as he could. She returned the embrace. "Hello, Mrs. Reynolds," he said, as they stood locked together.

Eva smiled. "I like the sound of that," she said.

Gus ran his hands through her hair untying the ribbon. Her hair fell in red swirls around her shoulders. "I love you, Mrs. Reynolds, and I always will," he said, as they kissed each other again.

Chapter 10
The Newlyweds

Gus and Eva returned to their home on the Reynolds' farm the next day. There were many tasks that needed to be completed. The house still had small things to be finished. The newlyweds had to become accustomed to living and working with one another. Gus had to continue to make a living, even more so since he now had a wife to provide for.

Gus returned to the river to fulfill his contract to deliver the timber rafts for Homer. Eva busied herself with setting her new house in order.

Gus was preparing to leave as Eva entered the bedroom where he was packing his clothes and other supplies. "How long do you think you'll be gone on this trip?" she asked, seating herself on the foot of the bed.

"Well, we've got about three more trips this spring. It'll take about a week to build each raft and deliver it to Doctor Town, if we take the train back each trip. That means I'll be home about once every five to seven days."

Gus finished tying his pack and sat beside her on the bed. Placing his arm around her, he hugged her gently. "I'm going to miss you, but I'm afraid it can't be helped. We've got to have the money to keep goin'."

Eva looked him in the eye and said, "I know. I'm not happy about it, but I guess I'll have to learn to live with it."

Gus leaned over and kissed her. Standing, he picked up his pack and turned to Eva. "I'm sorry, but hangin' around ain't gonna make it any easier."

Eva smiled ever so slightly, "You're right." She followed

Gus to the door and watched as he walked down the road toward his father's house.

Gus stopped at Alonzo's house momentarily. "Ma, I wonder if I could get you to look in on Eva once in awhile while I'm gone."

Susie looked at him with some concern. "Okay, son, I can remember what it was like to be a new wife with all the new things to become accustomed to. I'll be glad to help her feel welcome."

Gus paused for a second then added, "Don't tell her I asked. She might think I'm interferin', and that's not what I'm about."

"I won't mention it. Your Pa'll help, too. I'll warn him to keep mum."

"Thanks, Ma. I'd better be on my way."

Gus continued to the river north of the farm. Here lay the property of his Uncle Homer who harvested timber off and on, mostly to supplement his farm income. Easy access to the river from his land made shipping timber by the river economical.

"Well, I see you survived the weddin'," Homer joked as he met Gus, "I'd like to have been there, but it's hard to get away sometimes."

"Thanks, Uncle Homer. By the way I appreciate you lettin' me use your rig. It really looked spiffy at the weddin'."

"You're welcome, Son. Glad I could help. How's Eva?"

"She's fine. Kinda down, on account of me having to leave so soon, but I am, too."

"I understand that. You could take some more time at home if you want."

"I reckon not. We need the money. Besides, we have to get used to bein' apart, 'cause as long as I do this kind of work, we'll be apart for some time."

"I can't argue with that. Well, you ought to see her in about a week. We've about got your first raft ready and it don't take that long to deliver to Doctor Town. By the way, I've got one of your old partners to make this trip with you."

"Who's that?"

"Why don't you come on down to the raft and meet him?"

Gus followed Homer to the river's edge where men were putting together a raft. I'd better inspect it myself, Gus thought as he surveyed the work.

A grizzled worker, wearing a slouch felt hat and vest over homespun shirt with suspenders to hold up his pants, looked up from the task he was performing. "Gus, you old son-of-gun, how're you doin'?"

Gus recognized him immediately. "Felix, you bag of bones. You're a sight for sore eyes."

The men shook hands. "What brings you out on the river this time of year?" Gus inquired. "I thought you'd be gettin' ready for spring plantin'."

"It's most done. Ain't nothin' that oldest boy of mine can't handle. 'Sides I had to get away from the wife and kids for a spell. Know what I mean?"

"I don't reckon I do."

"Oh, that's right, you're a newlywed, ain't you? I hear tell you married that redheaded sister of young George Hester from up in Jeff Davis County."

"That's right. We was married last Sunday."

"Well, the new ain't wore off yet. Just you wait till you been married as long as me and my missus, then you'll know what I'm gettin' at."

"I'm not too sure about that, but I'll keep your words of wisdom in mind."

The raft would be ready to leave tomorrow. Homer usually sold his timber in Doctor Town because the price was about as good there as it was down river at Darien, and besides, it took less time to deliver and cost less to pay wages for raftsmen for a three-day versus a five-day trip.

Gus inspected the raft, as he usually did, for tight joints and other security reasons. His inspection completed, he gave direction for some adjustments he felt were needed and left the work to others, while he and Homer talked about how to handle the business at the end of the trip.

"You can just have the sawmill give you the usual bank draft for payment. I've got money to pay the hands so, I won't be needin' cash for this raft. Oh, and I've got some run money for you." Homer handed Gus a roll of bills. "Another thing, I want you to take the train back. We've got most of the logs cut for shipping this season, and I want to finish as quick as possible."

Gus put the money in a billfold that he carried strapped to his belt. "Okay, we'll shove off first light tomorrow. Let's get a bite to eat. I'm starved."

* * *

Eva turned back into the house. There was so much to do. Where should I start? She asked herself. One thing was certain, she had to stay busy and not worry about Gus. For one thing, he had gone on these trips dozens of times and knew how to take care of himself. Another, she told herself, worrying wouldn't help.

She decided to start in the kitchen. Curtains would surely brighten the windows, so she set about selecting some from those she had already made. After all, these were available, and she could always change them if she liked. That was one advantage of decorating your own house. Through the years, Eva would develop a talent for changing the appearance of her home by rearranging the furniture and changing the curtains, often from one window to another in a different room. If you didn't have much money, you had to learn to be creative.

Eva had hung one curtain when she heard a knock at the door. Susie stood there with a basket in her hand. "Hello, Mrs. Reynolds. Please come in," Eva said, as she opened the door.

"Child, you don't have to be so formal. Just call me Susie, or even Ma will be fine, if it's okay with you."

"Ma'll take some gettin' used to, but I'd like to call you Susie if that's okay."

"That's fine," Susie said, placing the basket on the dining table.

"Won't you have a seat?" Eva asked as she turned a dining chair around and offered it to Susie.

Susie seated herself and folded her hands in her lap. "I just come by to see if you needed anything."

Eva seated herself opposite her mother-in-law. "To tell the truth, I don't know. Everything's sort of muddled in my head. I don't know where to start. I was just tryin' to brighten up the place with some curtains."

Susie looked at the window where Eva had hung the curtain. "That's as good a place as any to start. Believe it or not, I remember what it was like to be a new bride. It's been more than thirty years, but I can remember how confusin' everything seemed to start with. Would you like me to send one of the girls to help you?"

"I can manage, but if you don't mind, I could use the company."

"Speakin' of company, why don't you have your evenin' meal with us till Gus gets back? It's awfully hard to cook for just one and we'd be glad to have you."

"Well, if it ain't too much trouble."

"Ain't no trouble at all. We'll just set another place at the table."

"That'd be nice."

"And another thing, if you don't care to stay here at the house by yourself at night, why not stay with us? You can have Gus's old room. It's private, and you won't be by yourself."

"Thank you, but I'd like to be home when Gus gets back."

"Do as you like. The offer's still good any time."

"I appreciate that."

Susie offered to help Eva with the kitchen. And, in a short while, the place was definitely more cheerful with new curtains at the windows.

Eva found Susie to be very supportive in the following days. They worked together on the house and in the garden and fields. There were a number of common interests that helped them to bond into a mother-daughter relation. In fact, this bonding might not have occurred as easily had Gus been present at all times.

Either Susie or Alonzo would call to see about Eva each day.

She would often accept Susie's standing invitation to meals and sometimes stay overnight with her mother-in-law. But mostly she worked on making the house more livable. Nevertheless, it seemed that Gus would never return. Her thoughts were of him almost constantly, even when she was performing some task that should have required her full attention.

* * *

Gus was just as mindful of his absence from Eva. He had begun the trip to Doctor Town the day after leaving her at home and he was always thinking of her. Felix often accused him of "Moonin'," daydreaming, about her.

"Boy, you sure ain't got your mind on your work," Felix said, as they floated downstream on a peaceful stretch of water.

"Why'd you say that?" Gus responded.

"The way you keep lookin' off out there like you was searchin' for the moon or somethin'."

"Oh, I was just thinkin'."

"Yep, and I'll bet I know what you was thinkin' about."

Gus grinned. "How'd you know that?"

"Boy, you got that far away look in yore eyes and the worst case of the lovesickness I've most ever seen."

"The heck you say. Is it that obvious?"

"Yep, but it'll pass. Just takes time. Maybe you shoulda stayed home awhile longer."

"I'll manage," Gus said, as he pulled the sweep to correct the course of the raft.

At night, Gus would settle down to sleep and dream. He always dreamed of Eva, and most of the time he thought about their future. His dreams were tempered with the reality of the world he lived in, but he always hoped for a bright future.

The raft was delivered to the sawmill, and he was on his way home at last. Only four days had passed, although it seemed like more. It seemed the train had never been so slow. Each time a switch had to be made, it took forever.

* * *

Eva had spent her day working in the house. In spite of her longing for Gus's return, she had actually accomplished a lot. Curtains now graced all the windows. Their bedroom was more cheerfully decorated, and the kitchen actually looked like you might be able to prepare a meal and find most of the things you needed to do it.

The sun was fading in the west when she heard the sound of horses approaching. Traffic on the road wasn't rare, but for some reason she wanted to see who it was. The horses stopped in front of the house. As she opened the door, a man dismounted from the wagon, picked up a bundle, slung it over his shoulder, and called as he strode toward the house, "Thanks for the ride, Uncle Homer."

"You're welcome," Homer responded. Then looking in Eva's direction added, "How are you, young lady?"

Eva smiled with delight as Gus came up the steps. "I'm fine, sir. How're you?"

"Never better. I brought Gus home for you. I'm tryin' to keep him out of trouble, you know," Homer joked.

Gus lowered his pack. "Yeah, I'll just bet you are. Who's gonna keep you straight?" He laughed.

"So long. See you Monday." Homer called as he slapped the reins and the horses started off down the road.

Gus reached for Eva, encircled her waist with his arms, and kissed her long and firmly on the mouth. Holding her in his arms he said, "My, how I've missed you."

Eva lay her head against his chest and listened to the beat of his heart. He smelled of wood smoke, unshaven and in need of a bath, but at the moment, she didn't care. It was enough to have him safe in her embrace again. "I missed you, too," she whispered. As they entered the house, Gus's pack was forgotten on the front porch.

A bath and change of clothes made Gus feel more presentable. Eva had taken advantage of the time to freshen up a bit herself. This chore taken care of, the couple met each other in the kitchen.

"What would you like for supper?" Eva asked.

Gus grinned, "Most anything I don't have to cook myself."

"Well, you can fetch me some stove-wood and I'll take care of the cookin'."

Gus brought in the wood, but he helped Eva with the meal preparation. They had finished their meal and were seated by the stove enjoying the warmth in the cool spring evening.

"Just two more trips, and we'll be able to spend more of our evenin's together," Gus said.

"I'm glad. It gets lonely here without you. Your Ma and Pa have been really nice, but it's not like havin' you around."

Eva had seated herself across from Gus in a dining chair. As he looked at her, he extended his hand to her. "Come here."

Eva took his hand as he pulled her to him and placed her on his lap. "Are you sure this chair'll hold both of us?" she teased.

"If it don't, we'll burn it for stove-wood and build one that will," Gus smiled as he squeezed Eva to him.

* * *

Sunday morning was a cool sunny spring morning. Gus and Eva had been invited to have their noon meal with Susie and Alonzo. They took advantage of the opportunity, and the family enjoyed a leisurely meal and conversation.

Gus and Alonzo retired to the front porch of the house while Eva helped Susie clear the table and wash the dishes. As they seated themselves in rocking chairs, Alonzo said, "Son, I've been thinkin' I ought to give you some fields of your own to work, now that you're a family man. You'll need some extra income, and you could grow a crop to help out."

"That's generous of you, Pa, but I'm not sure I'd be home enough to do the plowin'. What with me workin' the river like I've been."

"I thought about that, and I figure we'd share the work, but you could sell the crop for yourself. You can pay me back by workin' my fields when you have the time."

"Which field did you have in mind?"

"How about the back forty?"

"That sounds fine to me. Eva and I'd like to have a garden, too."

"Well, you can grow one of your own, if you're amind, but we can all share one, too."

"I know, but it's special to have your very own."

The ladies joined the men, and the conversation continued around the field and the future plans. The afternoon was perhaps half spent when Gus and Eva excused themselves to return to their house. Strolling up the road, they held hands and chatted. As they approached the house, they paused under the large live oak. A bench left there from the house raising gave them a comfortable outdoor seat in the shade of the tree.

"I'd not mind if this day lasted a bit longer," Gus said, placing his arm around Eva. "I'm not looking forward to leavin' you tomorrow."

"Let's not think about the leavin'. Let's concentrate on the time we have."

"Let's," Gus agreed.

* * *

Eva turned over in bed. Gus wasn't there. She was groggy with sleep, but she could hear him in the kitchen. The flickering light of the lamp cast his shadow across the floor as he made preparations to leave. Outside, the darkness still ruled.

"Why didn't you wake me? I'll fix you some breakfast," Eva said, as she walked into the kitchen pulling her robe around her.

"We don't have time for that. I'll just snack on some of these leftovers. I was goin' to let you sleep until I was ready to go."

"Do you have to leave so early? It's still dark outside."

"Yes. I'll need to be on the river as early as possible. There's plenty of starlight, and besides, I've walked those roads so many times; I can do it blindfolded."

Gus completed his preparations and turned to Eva. "You take care now," he said, as he hugged her and kissed her goodbye.

Gus left through the kitchen door. Eva decided it was too early to get up, so she went back to bed. The warmth and smell of Gus's body lingered under the bedcovers. She lay down where Gus had slept and was fast asleep, momentarily. The rising sun would awaken her later.

* * *

Gus made two more trips that spring, returning home for a day or so about once a week. Finally, the rafting season came to an end, and he could stay home and work on the farm. Farm work didn't seem quite so boring anymore. Eva was there beside him most of the time, and even when she wasn't present, she was never that far away.

"Whoa," Gus said, as he reined Doc to a stop at the end of the furrow in the back forty. Pulling a blue and white bandanna from his pocket, he wiped his brow and looked across the field. This field seemed like forty acres, even though it was much less, especially when you were working alone.

"Hello," a voice called from the vicinity of the big shade tree at the end of the field.

Gus hadn't seen anybody come into the field, which was unusual, since he was usually so alert. He wrapped the reins around the plow stock and walked toward the tree. Eva had been standing in the shade opposite him.

"Hello there, Beautiful. How in the world did you get here without me seein' you?"

"I found a pig trail through the woods and followed it."

"Oh, yeah. I'd forgot about that. Leave it to my girl to go explorin'. What brings you out here this time of day? Ain't nothin' wrong is there?"

"No. I Just thought you might like a fresh drink of water and a snack," Eva said, seating herself in the shade of the tree.

"I might at that," Gus joined her.

Eva handed him a small basket containing some leftover breakfast bacon and biscuits that she had heated and wrapped in a cloth to keep warm. "I thought you might like some company, too."

"I always enjoy your company," Gus said, biting off a chunk of biscuit and chewing it thoughtfully.

"Thank you," Eva said, perkily.

Gus looked out across the field, "We should be able to make a good crop if I can ever finish the plowin'."

"How much have you done?"

"I'm about half through. It'll take another day, I reckon."

"What are you plannin' to plant?"

"I thought about some cotton and corn. We can sell the cotton for cash, and the corn will come in handy for grits and meal and animal feed."

"That sounds sensible to me."

Gus finished the biscuit he was eating and took a long drink of water from the jug. "That was good, Mrs. Reynolds, but you had best go and let me get back to work or I'll forget what I'm supposed to be doin'. You are a wonderful distraction."

Eva grinned, "Why, thank you, Mr. Reynolds." She reached for him, and he held her and kissed her.

* * *

The crops were finally planted and now the battle with the weeds began. Gus and Eva would work side by side hoeing the cotton and corn. Gus never insisted that she help, but Eva was an outdoor person and delighted in being by Gus's side when she could.

The turpentine woods were a different story. This labor was so hard that most women didn't tackle it. Gus felt that this was definitely man's work. But he didn't have to worry, Eva felt the same way.

While Gus worked in the woods, Eva worked together with Susie to can vegetables for the winter. String beans, peas, and corn were staple items for canning. The canning process consisted of picking the produce from the field or garden, removing the hulls or snapping the peas or beans, and husking the corn and cutting it from the cob. Then the foods were packed into jars and cooked for hours over a hot stove, or maybe in the syrup boiler. The cooking not only preserved the food, but sealed the jars to prevent spoilage. This process made foods available for one to two years and sometimes longer.

Gus would finish a "dipping," a harvest of gum, from the trees, and haul it to the still. On some occasions, he would ask Eva to accompany him on the trip. They would spend some time shopping for small items for the house or perhaps buying material to make clothes. On rare occasions they might buy some ready made clothing.

August came and the cotton had to be picked. This was a laborious process. A cotton sack was prepared by taking a burlap bag and tying a strap to the two sides. The picker pulled this sack along behind as they picked the cotton by hand. When the bag was full, it was dumped into a sheet. The sheet usually consisted of four burlap bags sewn together.

A good picker could pick between two and three hundred pounds per day. Others struggled to harvest one hundred pounds. If someone worked for wages, their harvest was weighed at the end of the day, and they were either paid on the spot or a record of the weight was entered into a ledger for a later pay date. Most of the work was done by the family. When outside help was needed, the hands usually swapped work.

Gus was glad when the last of the cotton was loaded on the wagon in the field. He had been storing it in Alonzo's barn, but this load wouldn't have to be stored. He was taking it straight to market. Hauling the cotton was the easy part. Waiting to deliver at the gin was an opportunity to catch up on the latest gossip and farming talk.

Finally, the harvest was in, the cotton picked, the corn picked and stored, and the vegetables canned and dried. There would be a bit of time for socializing. Their social life consisted of church outings, neighborhood parties, barn raisings, and family reunions. Almost all events, except church, involved dancing or "frolickin'" as the locals called it. A fall favorite was "cane grinding."

"Uncle Buck's" was one of the best. People came from all

over to dance, drink cane juice, and party. Gus and Eva decided to attend this event. After all, they had been working hard and they felt they deserved a break.

For days now, Buck's family had been cutting and gathering the cane from the field. The grinding, or squeezing of the juice from the cane, was accomplished by rolling it between two drums fitted between two horizontal mounts. These drums were attached together by meshed gears. A boom atop one of the gears, mounted on an axle in the drum, was hitched to a draft animal, usually a mule or an ox, which pulled it in a circle rotating both drums. The juice flowed into a trough, and then into a tub or boiler where it was cooked to one thickness or another as the syrup maker desired.

There was plenty of work to be done, but there was usually dancing and other fun and games. These people had a talent for turning the most mundane task into an entertainment and work sharing time. These parties sometimes got rowdy because the cane squeezin's weren't the only drink being consumed. Corn squeezin's, alcohol made from corn, was also a popular drink. Depending on the host, the corn product might, or might not be allowed. Uncle Buck was known for refusing to permit drunkenness, but it didn't make his parties any less popular.

Gus and Eva danced several dances, some with other partners, but mostly with each other. It was good to relax after a hard season of work. Besides, they both knew Gus would soon return to the river and their time together would be more limited.

They finished a set and the caller was preparing to start the next dance. "Let's set a spell," Gus suggested.

"I'm ready. That last one wore me out."

They found a seat near the fire. The night air had taken on a fall chill making the fire a welcome haven. "Havin' a good time?" Gus asked.

"I am."

"Good. This has been a welcome relief for me, too."

Buck spotted the couple and sauntered over to speak. "Well, and how are the newlyweds?"

Gus looked up. "We're doin' just fine, Uncle Buck. Some party you got goin' tonight."

"Yeah, thank you. It's better than some. At least, everyone seems to be enjoying theirselves without any rowdiness. How was your crop this year?"

"It turned out okay. We didn't get as much for the cotton as I hoped, but I reckon that's to be expected."

"You gonna work the river this winter?"

"I reckon so. I ain't exactly sure where, though. I been so busy farming, I ain't had time to look for a winter job."

"Well, you be careful. That's a might pretty bride you got there. Wouldn't want to leave her all alone, you know."

Gus wondered at this remark. He said, "You're right about that."

Buck walked away and Eva said, "Why'd he say that?"

"What?"

"That thing about leavin' me all alone."

"Just makin' a joke, I reckon."

It might have been a joke to Buck, but it expressed one of Eva's worst fears. The fear that Gus might leave and never return.

Chapter 11
The Firstborn

Colder weather was here. It was time to go to work at winter jobs. Gus hadn't had time to hunt work on the river, but he didn't worry. The demand for river pilots was fairly high, and he seldom had any trouble finding employment.

Meantime, it had been some time since Eva had visited her home and family. With this in mind, Gus and Eva hitched up a team of horses and made the journey to Jeff Davis County. Arriving late in the afternoon, they found the Hester family busy with their end-of-day chores.

As Gus reined in the team in front of the gate, some of the younger children came running down the hall shouting at the top of their lungs. "Eva's home! Eva's Home!"

The family converged on the house from the barn and various parts of the yard and field. They all greeted Gus and Eva enthusiastically; the sisters hugging each other, and the brothers speaking and then shaking hands with Gus.

"I'll put up the team and wagon for you," George volunteered.

"Thanks," Gus answered.

Everyone else headed for the house. They congregated in the sitting room. Everybody wanted to talk at once. Finally, they began to take turns.

"Goodness, child, how you've changed," Annie said. "Married life seems to agree with you."

Eva teased Gus. "I reckon I've put on some weight. You see Gus. He's skinny as a rail, 'cause he won't eat my cookin', and I have to eat it or throw it to the hogs." Everybody laughed, even

Gus.

"She only burns the biscuits seven days a week," he cracked.

Annie had other concerns on her mind. "It'll be supper time soon. Why don't you men stay here, and me and the girls will go out to the kitchen and fix us a meal."

There was no disagreement; so the women left the men alone and went to prepare supper. "Lord, child, it's good to see you. Tell me what all you've been up to," Annie said, as they exited the room.

Bill pushed back in his chair, crossed his legs and faced Gus. "Son, what you up to? I trust you had a good crop this year."

"The crop was fine," Gus answered. "I'm kind of between jobs at the moment. I've not had time to find winter work."

"I don't reckon you know that Uncle Sebe is cutting some timber down on his place near Town's Ferry?"

"No, sir, I didn't."

"I've been thinkin' about workin' down there some this winter myself. Most of the farm work's done until spring, and I don't want to set on my hands the whole winter. Would you be interested in workin' with us?"

"Sure, sounds good to me."

"Why don't you let Eva stay here and visit with her Ma while you and I take a trip down and see what's goin' on."

* * *

The next day Bill, Gus, and George took leave of the family and drove to Towns Bluff on the Altamaha River. Sure enough, the logging camp had been set up, and a few workers were already busy cutting trees to be shipped down river. These were hardwoods and had to be handled differently. Hardwoods are too dense to float when cut green, so the loggers girth the tree, strip the bark from around the tree, allowing it to die. As it dies, it loses moisture and becomes less dense resulting in a log that will float.

As they drove into the camp, Bill spied one of the Halls. Reining his horses in, he called, "Hey, who's in charge here?"

"I reckon that'd be me."

"I know you're one of Sebe's boys, but I don't remember your name."

"It's Travis."

"Oh, yeah, now I remember. Didn't you used to work the railroad?"

"Yep. It got to be too much of a hassle."

"You hired a raft pilot yet?"

"Not particularly. I've got some men that could maybe get by, but I could use a first-rate hand if I could get him."

"I'd like you to meet my son-in-law, Gus Reynolds. He's one of the best. Been raftin' on this river for quite a while."

"Glad to meet you, Gus. Say, didn't you raft for the Fletcher outfit out of Lumber City a couple of years back?"

Gus dismounted from the wagon seat and grasped Travis's extended hand. "That's right."

"I hear you did a fine job for them, even saved a man's life that got snake bit."

"I just did the best I could with what I had to work with."

Travis grinned, "That's good enough for me. When can you start?"

"It'll take a couple of days. I didn't come prepared to go to work right away."

"You've got a job. Just let me know when you get back."

The men chatted about timber work in general, as Travis showed them the camp and told them what he wanted to accomplish during the current logging season. Bill, Gus, and George left with the understanding that they could all go to work any time they were ready.

* * *

When they returned to the Hester's home, Eva didn't take the news with a great deal of enthusiasm. Gus tried to help her understand. "I'll be nearby most of the time, and you can stay with your Ma while I'm workin', if that's okay with you and her. Your Pa's gonna be workin' with us, and I'll see you as often as I can."

"You don't mean Pa's goin' down river with you?"

"I don't think so, but he sure could if he wanted."

"What about our house? Who's gonna look out for things there?"

"Ma and Pa'll help us with that."

"Are you goin' to return your Pa's team?"

"Yes. We'll make a trip home and return with what we need to get us by. Your Pa's promised to help. This might even get us enough money to buy our own horse and wagon."

Eva agreed somewhat reluctantly.

Bill, Annie, Gus, and Eva had a conference to work out the details, and Gus and Bill were soon on their way to return with the things Gus and Eva would need for an extended stay. They returned the next day, and all seemed in order for the departure to the logging work.

"We'll be back about once a week," Gus reassured Eva.

"I'll be okay. It just seems strange, not having you around."

"Don't worry, everything's gonna be fine."

* * *

Bill, Gus, and George left for Town's Bluff the next day. Bill had provided several comforts, among them, a small tent and some blankets. All in all, this was the best equipped Gus had ever been, and he thought he was living in luxury.

The Hall family shipped their timber to Doctor Town mostly, so a raft trip and return by train usually required about six days. Enough timber for one raft had been felled by the time Gus returned to the camp with Bill and George. Gus set about building a raft almost immediately. Even with the dry condition of the trees, the hardwoods floated low in the water. Rafters would often get their feet wet, and this could cause health problems. Respiratory disease from exposure was not uncommon.

The first raft was ready in a couple of days. About the time Gus was ready to shove off, Felix showed up asking for a job.

"I know him. He's a good rafter," Gus told Travis. "I'd like to have him work with me, if that's all right?"

"Pick out whoever you want. You're the boss on the raft."

Gus decided he'd take George with him, too. The three left early the next morning. The run to Doctor Town was done without any significant difficulty. The train brought them back to Hazlehurst, and they had completed the trip in almost record time.

Gus found the work pleasant and rewarding. It was nice to have a crew that you could call on and expect good results. He was given a free hand in his work, and he always accomplished more when his employer trusted him to do his job.

* * *

Meanwhile, Eva found it felt strange to be home with her mother again. She decided a visit would be fine in the future, but one house wasn't big enough for two women who each were accustomed to having things her own way. She also found that children were still children, and that her mother expected much the same of her as before she had married.

On one of Gus's trips home, he and Eva discussed their future. It seemed to her that they needed to return home. She had been away too long and was sure the house was simply falling apart without her to watch over things.

"I think I should go home for a while and see about things."

Gus thought for a minute. "I think you're right. We ought to see about our things. You can stay home if you want. It won't be any trouble to come by home on my way back. We can see each other then."

Gus sent word to Travis that he would be delayed shortly, and he and Eva left the next day to return home. To her relief, Eva found that things at home were pretty much as she had left them. It was good to be home under her own roof. She enjoyed visiting with her mother, but she had become head of her own house and liked that role much better.

Gus made regular trips to Doctor Town throughout the winter, and after each trip, he returned by way of his home in Baxley. Eva stayed home more now and went to visit with her mother mostly on special occasions, such as Christmas. The winter was fairly mild that year and the work on the river proceeded at a good pace. Gus was able to set aside some money for things he felt he needed to buy.

Spring came and the world began to take on a bright new look. The weather was unusually mild and the rains were sufficient to sustain the water level needed for rafting, but not too bothersome to work at a more or less steady pace.

Gus, George, and Felix were floating peacefully along on the river. There wasn't much to do at the moment. The atmosphere was relaxed, and the spring day was unusually warm. Felix, who always wore long johns under his clothing, had decided the weather was warm enough to shed some clothing. He removed everything, except his underwear.

Gus, who was at least modest in his dress, discovered the action and addressed the problem as he saw it. "Felix, what in the hell do you think you're doin'?"

"What you talkin' about?"

"Your clothes. What're you doing with your clothes off?"

"What do it look like? I'm coolin' off."

"Man, get your pants on."

"How come?"

"There's people on this river."

Felix spat a stream of tobacco juice into the water and watched it dissipate in the flowing liquid, "So?"

"So, there's women fishing along the banks."

"What about it?"

Gus's temper was beginning to rise. "Dammit, Felix, there are respectable women on this river."

Felix thought for a minute. "Huh," he grunted, "they can't be respectable."

"How's that?"

"If they was respectable, they wouldn't be on the river."

Clearly, Gus and Felix's logic was at counter purpose on this subject. In one form or another, they would disagree on this topic more than once.

* * *

The logging season was over. Gus had had a good winter, and together with the money he had been able to set aside from last season's crop, he now had enough to make some major purchases. He and Eva shopped for some living room furnishings and other household goods, but his main purpose was to provide them with some transportation of their own.

The first priority was to buy a horse. The animal had to be a good drafter, but Gus hoped to find one that also had some aesthetic qualities. He hesitated to patronize stock traders, since he had found most of them to be shysters. They would take an animal in trade that they knew to be sick or have some other defect, then trade him as first rate stock to the unwary buyer. Never was the axiom, "Let the buyer beware" more appropriate than now.

Through the grapevine Gus learned of a farmer who had a horse for sale. He made the trip to inspect the animal. Arriving about the middle of the afternoon, he introduced himself and stated his business.

"He's out to the barn," the farmer said, standing with his thumbs hooked to his overall gallows. "Come on down and look him over."

Gus followed the owner to an old unpainted barn which must have been at least fifty years old. It was in need of repairs. Boards had fallen from the sides where the wind had torn them loose, or where they had simply rotted. I hope his animals are better kept than his barn. Gus thought, as they entered the lot gate near the barn.

"That's him. The one with the stockin' foots," the farmer said, pointing to a young horse. The animal was beautiful. Gus guessed him to be about eighteen hands high with strong muscular shoulders and a straight back. Approaching the animal carefully, Gus checked his hooves and then inspected his teeth.

"He seems pretty gentle. Is he broke for a wagon?"

"Yesir. He'll pull a wagon, plow or even take a saddle."

"Mind if I ride him?"

"Help yoreself. I got a old saddle in the barn if you want."

The saddle was fetched and placed on the horse's back. He seemed a bit skittish, but Gus soothed him with a soft voice as he tightened the cinch. "Whoa, boy. Easy fellow. You and I are going to get better acquainted."

Satisfied that the saddle was firmly in place, Gus called to the farmer, "Open the gate. I want to try him on the road."

As the gate swung back, Gus placed a foot in the stirrup and mounted as the horse moved forward. The horse reacted to the unfamiliar weight on his back and bucked a couple of times. Gus was expecting it, so he was able to keep his seat without any difficulty. Gus gave the horse his head and let him move at his own pace until he cleared the gate, then he urged him into a trot, and then a run for perhaps a quarter of a mile.

At the end of the sprint, the horse was breathing a bit hard, but he soon recovered. He needs more exercise, Gus thought. Gus walked him back to the barn running his hands over his muscles. A good brushing would help him look better, he thought.

Gus dismounted and wrapped the reins around a lot post. "How much you askin'?"

"I figger he's worth about seventy-five."

Gus looked thoughtful. "How about sixty?"

The farmer scratched his head and spat on the ground. "What'd you say to seventy?"

"I'd say sixty-five."

"Tell you what, I'll throw in the saddle for seventy."

Gus thought for a moment. He didn't think he'd actually need the saddle, but he didn't own one, so he said, "I'll take it."

The farmer turned toward the house. "Come on up and I'll give you a bill-of-sale."

As they walked up the hill to the house, Gus remembered to ask, "What do you call him anyhow?"

"Oh, I call 'im 'Socks'."

Socks turned out to be a good investment. Gus still had to borrow a wagon from Alonzo, but he could now make a trip without taking one of the farm animals away from their duty. Socks was easily trained to work with other horses as a team and became a good work animal.

* * *

The crops were gathered in the fall, and Gus got a good price for his cotton. Things were really looking up. He didn't owe any money and had actually come out with enough to buy a one-horse wagon. He and Eva were in the field loading corn that had been picked and laid in piles.

"I think I'll try and find us a wagon next week."

Eva stood up with an arm load of corn, walked to the wagon and heaved it over the side. "It would be nice to have our own. Then we could go somewhere without askin' to borrow your Pa's."

Gus relieved himself of his load and turned to Eva. Her face looked pale, and she seemed short of breath. Gus stepped to her side and caught her as she almost fell.

"What's wrong?"

"I don't know. I feel weak. I'll just rest a minute."

Gus eased Eva to the ground and seated himself beside her still holding her. "Is that better?"

"Yes. Much better. Thank you."

Gus looked worried. "You shouldn't be doin' this work. I've noticed you. You've been pale more than usual lately."

"I'll be okay. I just need to rest."

"Here, let me get you on the wagon."

Gus picked her up and placed her on the wagon seat. "We're goin' to the house. No argument."

Eva smiled weakly. "Don't be silly. I'm all right."

Gus picked up the reins, and Socks moved obediently off at a walk. "I ought to be ashamed workin' you like that."

"I volunteered, remember."

* * *

Dr. Bratcher finished his examination of Eva. She wasn't overly fond of doctors. The less she saw of one the better she thought. The doctor laid his stethoscope aside.

"Well?" Eva asked.

"I don't think it's anything serious."

"That's what I told Gus. What is it?"

"Oh, you'll be over it in about nine months."

"What?"

"You're pregnant, Mrs. R."

Eva blushed. "Say that again."

"You're pregnant. You're gonna have a baby."

"How soon?"

"Hard to tell. My guess would be about five to six months."

Gus could hardly contain himself. He was going to be a father. This was a totally new experience. Everyone congratulated him and Eva and always wanted to know if they wanted a boy or a girl. Gus thought the question was ridiculous. It didn't matter what he wanted, the choice wasn't up to him. He and Eva decided the best answer to this query was, "Yes."

Gus absolutely refused to let Eva work in the fields. She protested. This was probably their first real argument, but he was adamant and she finally gave in. It wasn't worth the fuss.

There were new priorities at the Reynolds' house. Eva wanted to get ready for the baby. The quandary was, how to plan for a baby when you didn't know if it was a boy or a girl. Gus and Eva decided they should pick two names, one of each. Gus wanted to name a son John Henry. Eva wasn't too fond of the name, but she said it would be okay if he'd let her name their daughter.

Eva asked Gus if he could build a cradle. He agreed, and the work was done in short order. The result wasn't too elaborate, but it was functional. Eva completed the work with clothing and pillows for the bed. Now she would be able to keep the baby near her any time of day.

Eva also made clothing for the baby. Babies were usually clothed in dresses regardless of their sex. White was a neutral color and most often used for newborns. The tradition of blue for boys and pink for girls could only be carried out in families that were well-to-do.

The neighborhood ladies made Eva presents of cloth and other baby items she would need. The grandparents were excited as well, and got involved when they could. Susie was nearby, so she had the most influence on Eva, including some old wives tales.

During one of their conferences about parenting, Susie and Eva were working in the kitchen when Eva reached up to place something in a cabinet. "Don't do that!" Susie admonished.

"For heaven's sake, why not?"

"Cause you'll wrap the cord around the baby's neck and choke it."

Eva didn't know quite how to respond to this so she held her peace and let Susie give her elderly advice. It had occurred to Eva that most of these ideas had no foundation in fact, but she wasn't prepared to argue the point. This was just one of many pieces of advice she received during her pregnancy.

* * *

Gus worked the river again that winter, leaving Eva for days at a time. He usually tried to see her at least once each week. Meanwhile, he asked his mother to look after her for him. The periods of absence seemed longer to Eva than they had as a new bride. Each time Gus returned, she greeted him with gladness and rejoiced that he was near her again.

"It's good to have you home," Eva said, as they snuggled in front of the fire one cold rainy winter evening.

"It's great to be home," Gus said, as he stroked her hair and kissed her cheek.

"Maybe it'll snow, so you can stay home."

"That'd be nice. Stayin' home, I mean. But it sure won't buy the groceries."

"We don't buy that many groceries."

"You're right."

"Gus?"

"What?"

"Sometimes, I'm afraid."

"Afraid of what honey? Bein' a ma?"

"Yes. But I can't help but wonder if you'll be here when the baby comes."

Gus hugged her and kissed her on the mouth. "Don't you worry. I wouldn't miss it for the world."

"I know you want to be here, but what if you're on the river and can't be here?"

"That's always possible, but I'm not goin' to leave you when it's time for the baby to come."

"I love you."

"I love you, too."

The month of March came and went. The baby still had not decided to face the light of the world. Eva felt that she was as large as an elephant, and very unattractive. She often asked Gus if he still loved her. She needed to be told that her appearance didn't cause her to be loved any less. Gus reassured her that she was still beautiful to him, and he meant every word.

April arrived, and Gus was preparing to pilot one more raft after spending a couple of days at home. He and Eva had gone to bed, and he had fallen asleep when he heard her call him and felt her hand on his shoulder. "Gus! Wake up. I think it's time."

"Time for what?"

"The baby's comin'."

Gus wiped the sleep from his eyes and sat up in bed. "I'll get Ma."

"Okay, but you'd better get the doctor, too."

"Don't worry."

Gus was out of bed and pulling his pants on. He stuffed his shirttail in his pants and pulled on his boots, giving them a half lace instead of the usual full lace and tie. He made a dash for the door and almost fell out the steps when he suddenly realized it was raining. Turning back into the house, he retrieved his slicker and exited again.

Socks was standing asleep in his stall when Gus threw open the door and reached for the bridle. He whinnied and nudged Gus's hand expecting a treat. Gus threw the saddle on and tightened the cinch. In a moment, he was on his way to the main farm house.

Susie woke to the sound of knocking on the bedroom door. She turned over in bed and shook Alonzo. "Pa! There's somebody at the door."

Alonzo grunted and turned to face Susie. "Who could it be?"

"Ma! It's me. Gus."

"Just a minute."

"Ma. I need you quick. Eva's in labor."

Susie pulled on a robe as she stood up. "You go get the doctor, son. I'll go to Eva directly."

"Thanks, Ma." Gus turned and bounded back into the night.

Socks was in good condition and it was a good thing. He and Gus must have covered the five miles to Dr. Bratcher's house in Baxley in record time.

Dr. Bratcher's office was an addition to his house. He made house calls regularly and sometimes was hard to find, but tonight he was home.

Gus pounded on the door of the house. "Doc! Doc! Wake up!"

A light came on in the house as Dr. Bratcher struck a match and lit a kerosene lamp. "Hold your horses. I'm a comin'."

The door opened to reveal Gus standing in the drizzling rain. His hat was slouched from the moisture and his face was wet and glistened in the lamp light. Dr. Bratcher held the door open. "Come in, young man."

Gus stepped inside, dripping water all over the floor.

"What can I do for you, young feller?"

Gus caught his breath. "It's my wife Doc. Her baby's comin'."

"Okay, calm down, son. I'll be with you momentarily."

Dr. Bratcher returned to his bedroom. Gus stood feeling like a waterfall as the water dripped from his hat and slicker puddling on the floor.

After what seemed an eternity to Gus, Doc returned, dressed for the inclement weather. "I'll just be another minute. Have to get my bag," he said, as he opened the door to his office and disappeared. He was back shortly.

"How'd you get here?"

"I rode my horse."

"Well, why don't you turn him in my stable and ride with me in my car? You won't be able to keep up otherwise."

Gus didn't argue. Socks didn't mind being left behind. The moment he realized he wasn't out in the rain anymore, he shook his mane. The water flew everywhere. Gus had enough forethought to relieve him of the burden of his saddle and bridle.

Under the shelter on the other side of the barn, Doc's car was spitting and complaining as he warmed it up. Gus swung into the passenger seat. "Let's go."

Doc let out on the clutch and the car jerked forward and splashed its way into the street. The cloth top kept some of the rain off, but not much. Water covered the two-piece windshield and dripped onto the dash of the car as they sped into the rain. Gus swore they must have been traveling twenty miles per hour.

Gus hung on as the car turned a curve and headed down the main road toward the farm. Doc looked over at Gus. Gus would have preferred Doc keep his eyes on the road. "This your first?" Doc asked, conversationally.

"Yeah."

"I thought so. You got all the symptoms of a new Pa."

Gus didn't say anything.

"You know, I been doctorin' for near thirty years now, and I've noticed somethin'."

"What that, Doc?"

"Babies. They're never born when it's convenient. No sir, if it's rainin' or snowin' or cold they're gonna come. It's most always the middle of the night, too."

The car hit a hole and almost bounced Gus out of the seat. Water splashed on him and wet him thoroughly. "Sorry about that. The fenders on this jalopy wasn't made for this kind of road."

Doc steered to the right as they forded Ten-Mile Creek. The car began to spit and sputter. Gus thought it was going to stall in the run of the creek, but somehow it recovered and chugged its way to the opposite bank.

* * *

The baby was definitely on its way. Eva lay on her bed. The contractions were getting closer. Susie sat beside her and wiped her forehead with a cloth. Eva gave a groan of pain and caught her breath as another contraction gripped her body.

Susie soothed her, "Now just hang in there; Gus will be here with the doctor before you know it."

Eva grimaced, "This young'un can't come too soon to suit me."

The sound of an automobile could be heard outside, and footsteps sounded on the front porch. The next moment the door opened to reveal Gus and Dr. Bratcher. Doc shed his rain gear and opened his bag. Retrieving his stethoscope, he approached the bed and began to examine Eva's abdomen. He paused, looked at Gus, and said, "We'll call you if we need you."

Gus couldn't see why he should leave the room, but he took the hint and retreated to the kitchen. Alonzo was there. He had built a fire in the stove and had a pot of coffee steaming.

"Sit down, Son. There ain't much we can do now. You fetched the doctor. He can handle it from here."

Gus stood near the stove and warmed himself. The heat was a welcome relief from the cold wet rain.

Alonzo looked at his son and realized he was soaked to the skin. "You might want to get out of them wet clothes," he prompted.

For the first time Gus looked at his clothes. He was as wet as if he had been dunked in the river. Some dry clothes might feel good at that. "Thanks, Pa. I'll be right back."

"Take your time. There ain't no hurry."

A few minutes later Gus returned in dry clothes and hung his slicker on a peg near the door. He poured himself a cup of coffee and sipped it. Then seating himself across the table from Alonzo, he slowly drank from the cup.

Time dragged on. It seemed the night would last forever. Gus would pace the floor, discover that he was pacing, and sit again. Outside, the rain grew more fierce as the wind blew it against the window panes.

It must have been dawn, but it was impossible to tell. The sky was covered with clouds and the rain continued to fall. Doc stepped into the kitchen, poured himself a cup of coffee, and looked at Gus.

Gus couldn't contain himself. "Well! Is everything okay?"

"Everything's fine. It won't be long now."

"Can I see her?"

"I reckon. But just a minute."

Gus entered the room and knelt by the bed grasping Eva's hand. "How're you doin', girl?"

Eva smiled weakly. "I'm all right. This young'un has a mind of its own though."

"I'm right here, just like I promised."

"Thank you, Darling."

"You'd best go now," Doc said, gently, as he touched Gus on the shoulder. Gus kissed Eva on the lips, released her hand, and exited the room.

Some time later, Doc entered the kitchen and said, "Congratulations, you are the father of a strong healthy baby girl."

Gus grinned like a mule eating briers and shouted, "Yippee!"

Susie came through the door with a bundle in her arms. Gus peered over her shoulder at the baby. "Ain't she the prettiest thing you ever saw?" Susie asked.

Gus looked at the wrinkled features of his daughter. "I don't know. She looks powerful ugly to me. Doc, what do you think?"

Doc knew better than to get in the middle of this argument although he thought all newborns were ugly. "She's an exceptionally fine lookin' child," he replied.

"Can I hold her?" Gus asked.

"Here, be careful," Susie handed her to Gus.

Gus gazed at the face of his daughter with all the pride a new father could exhibit and said, "Welcome to the world, Lorene Reynolds. It's good to get to know you."

Chapter 12
The Vigil

Lorene grew like a weed during the spring and summer. Except for usual bouts with colic and other infant maladies, she was quite a normal baby. There were, of course, times when she needed doctoring. Eva took care of this for the most part, with help and advice from her mother-in-law, and sometimes from other well-meaning women, who dispensed their advice freely. Eva discovered that one of the things a new mother has to learn is--what advice to keep and what to discard. She learned that everybody considered themselves experts on child rearing, but in fact were really trying something to see if it worked, then trying something else if it didn't.

On one occasion, Eva consulted Dr. Bratcher, although she was reluctant to do so. "So what seems to be the problem?" he asked.

"She seems to be more fretful than usual, and I think she may have a touch of fever," Eva said, as she held her and rocked her gently in her arms.

"Let's have a look at her."

Eva laid Lorene on the examining table.

"What have you tried?" Doc asked as he began to check her with his stethoscope.

"I've tried just about anything that anyone has mentioned. I've had all the free advice I can use, now I'm ready to pay for some."

Doc listened to her heart and lungs, then checked her pulse at various points of the body. Her eyes were examined. He finished some other checks and straightened up from the table. "I can't find anything obvious. Perhaps she's teething. It might be I could give her some paregoric, in small doses, until her system fights off whatever's botherin' her."

He measured out a small bottle of the drug and handed it to Eva. "How much?" she asked.

"Um, let's see. I reckon fifty cents for the exam and a quarter for the medicine."

Eva searched her purse and found two coins. Placing them in his hand, she said, "Thank you," and left the office.

* * *

The summer wore on. Gus was busy with his usual summer chores of plowing and turpentining, but was able to spend a good deal of time with his family. He took delight in his baby girl. Holding her, he would talk to her and play with her and marvel at the gift of life in her body and the joy and spontaneity of her smile. He helped with her when he could, but changing diapers and feeding were Eva's job exclusively.

Eva found that she had to divide her time more now. Lorene demanded time, but she and Gus found time to be together, although not as much as they had before. She and Gus easily made room for the new family member, and after awhile, it seemed Lorene had always been a part of their lives.

Lorene had aunts and uncles who were always around, so she learned all the little things that so many people think are cute at an early age. Her grandparents, Susie and Alonzo, were also very proud of their new granddaughter and took every opportunity to see her and spoil her as much as they could. It seems grandparents have a way of allowing their grandchildren to get away with things that they would never have allowed their children to do.

Gus and Eva's social life, which had never been too active, was not affected much by Lorene. There were always baby sitters around in the person of aunts and uncles. When they went to some social gathering, children were most often a part of the group. Admiring friends and relatives would help by entertaining Lorene. Eva especially found this helpful. She had learned that a mother needs a rest from constantly watching her baby. There may be unlimited love, but there is a limit to the strain on the body and nerves of any mother.

The summer passed, and fall arrived with the usual harvest to be completed. Eva had been very happy during this season. Gus had been home, and the baby had really made them a family, but winter was coming, and she dreaded the thought of being separated from Gus. It was true that he was never gone for any extended period, not more than a week, if possible, but even these absences seemed too long.

Gus left for the swamp and worked there on a somewhat regular basis. Eva and Lorene were alone except for the usual visits of the family. Eva did find that she had less time to think about Gus's absence since she now had to see about Lorene and had her for company. She would often talk to her daughter as if they were carrying on a conversation. As a result, Lorene began to try to talk somewhat earlier than most firstborn children.

* * *

One day while Eva was busy working in the kitchen, she heard the sound of an approaching vehicle. This was not uncommon since people often passed by the house on their way to town and other destinations. The wagon stopped and a voice called out, "Hello. Anybody home?"

Peering through the front window, Eva thought to herself, oh my God, a peddler!

Peddlers were common in these times. Most of them were considered crooks, and some people refused to deal with them, but they did bring goods to remote areas that folks would not have had access to otherwise. Eva really wasn't afraid, but she did have some concern lest this stranger try to harm her or Lorene. She thought of staying in the house hoping he would simply leave, but then it occurred to her that she would be rid of him sooner if she faced him and sent him on his way.

The merchant was not easily discouraged. He waited a moment and dismounted from his wagon, walked through the gate, and knocked on the door. The door opened to reveal a red-haired woman holding a broom in one hand.

"Good day, ma'am. Allow me to introduce myself. My name is Jonas Peabody, and I'm here to show you my wares. I've got the finest selection south of the Mason-Dixon line, and they're just a waitin' for you to look 'em over."

Eva hesitated for a second, which was a mistake, so Jonas continued, "I got pots and pans for your kitchen. I got medicines that'll cure whatever ails you, and most any thing you could want."

Eva found her voice, "I don't see how you could have anything I'd want on that one wagon. Besides, I don't need anything right now, and if I did, I couldn't afford it."

Jonas reached up and removed his hat, "Why, ma'am, my prices are the best around. You can't even get these things for this low a price in the finest store in town. Besides, it don't cost nothin' to look."

Eva saw that getting rid of this smooth talker wasn't going to be as easy as she had hoped. She was trying to think of another objection when she spied someone standing in the road next to the gate. "Why, Mr. Reynolds! How nice to see you."

Alonzo had approached the house on foot and quietly watched as the exchange was unfolding between Eva and the peddler. He was leaning on the gatepost taking in the scene.

Jonas swallowed and turn to look at the newcomer. Undaunted, he said, "Good day to you, Sir. To whom do I have the pleasure of speakin'? Are you, perhaps, the man of the house?"

Alonzo spat a stream of chewing tobacco on the bottom of the gatepost, wiped his mouth with his hand, and said, "It ain't none of your business who I am. But no, I ain't the man of the house. I do have a right to see that you don't pester this young woman, though."

Jonas' face showed a look of surprise as he responded, "Pester? Sir, I wasn't meanin' to pester anybody. Least of all this young lady. May I interest you in some of my wares?"

Alonzo measured Jonas with his eyes, looking him up and

down. "I don't reckon we need anything today."

Jonas was persistent, but he wasn't stupid. He was starting to get the message that peddlers weren't welcome at this house, especially himself. He decided to bow out gracefully. "Well, I'll be goin', seein' as how you folks seem to have all you need right now. Maybe I'll drop by next time I'm in the neighborhood," he said, as he placed his hat on his head and retreated through the gate, passing within arm's reach of Alonzo.

Alonzo watched him mount the wagon and pick up the reins. "Maybe?" he said, as Jonas slapped the reins on his horse's back and moved off down the road. Alonzo watched him retreat, then turned to Eva. "You all right?"

"Yes. Thank you very much. I don't know what I'd have done if you hadn't come along."

Alonzo grinned, "Well, I don't know if you thought about it, but it appears to me he would have left here with a sore head."

Eva looked puzzled, "What?"

"I figured you was gonna whack him with that broom."

Eva looked at the potential weapon in her hand and blushed. "I don't know if I would have or not."

"Well, there ain't no way to tell what might have been. You just need to be prepared for anything when dealin' with people like him. To tell the truth, I just don't trust them fellers. Like as not, he won't be back. If he does though, you be ready for him."

"Thank you. I will. Goodness, I forgot to ask, what brings you here this time of day?"

"I just wanted to see my granddaughter and see if there was anything you needed. I know it's tough sometimes with Gus bein' gone so much."

Eva heard a cry from the bedroom signaling that Lorene was awake. This was fortunate because her grandpa had been known to awaken her in the middle of a nap just to hold her and talk to her.

Eva turned to enter the house, "Why don't you come in and visit with Lorene for a spell while I see if I can find us something to drink. What would you like?"

"I think a glass of buttermilk would hit the spot, if you got any," Alonzo said, as he climbed the steps and entered the house. He went to the bedroom and lifted Lorene from her cradle and held her close to him talking to her. She responded with a smile and gurgled with pleasure at the sound of his voice.

Eva came into the sitting room with a glass of milk and a cup of coffee. She placed the milk by the chair for Alonzo and seated herself in a chair nearby.

Alonzo tickled the baby on her stomach much to her delight, "What in the world you been feedin' this young'un? She's gained a ton since I held her last."

Eva knew he was teasing so she went along with the joke. "Just the usual. She's startin' to eat from the table, and sometimes she can't seem to get enough."

"That's good. She'll grow and be healthy."

"I just wish Gus was here to see her grow."

Alonzo shifted Lorene on his lap and looked at Eva. "I know what you mean. His Ma frets all the time when he ain't around. But you got to understand how it is with him. He's got a sort of fever that keeps drawin' him back to that river. I reckon it's almost like he had a mistress, except it's the river."

"Well, I can be thankful it's not another woman."

"I don't think there's any danger of that. But he's got river mud in his veins, and he just can't stay away."

"I know what you mean. He seems restless when he's workin' on the farm."

"Always has been. Can't wait to get back to that river."

* * *

Christmas came, and Gus was home for a few days. He did his best to make the occasion joyful for Eva and the baby. He always tried to buy something practical for Eva, but he sometimes indulged her with some trinket or other. This was Lorene's first Christmas, so her stocking wasn't too hard to fill. A small toy was sufficient.

The next year came and went with the usual routine. Lorene

grew rapidly and started walking, which made it possible for her to get into everything she could. One day Eva missed her. She wasn't making any noise, so it was impossible to tell where she was simply by listening. After a while Eva heard a noise in the kitchen and decided she'd better investigate.

She found Lorene standing on a chair at the dining table. On the table was a basket of eggs that had been gathered earlier that day. Lorene was systematically picking up one egg at a time and dropping it on the floor, smiling with delight when it hit the floor and splattered.

"Young lady, what do you think you're doing?" Eva said firmly, as she caught her under the arms and lifted her from the chair, swatting her on the bottom with her hand.

Lorene looked at her with innocent eyes and pointing to the floor said, "Egg."

"What's left of them," Eva sighed.

The basket held perhaps half of the eggs that were gathered earlier. Eva resigned herself to cleaning up the mess while she admonished her daughter not to repeat the offense.

This was just one of many of Lorene's climbing episodes. She had an insatiable curiosity and found her way to places Eva would have not thought possible. Once Eva found her on top of her bedroom dresser. She had pulled the drawers open and used them for steps to accomplish her climb.

* * *

That fall, Eva also learned that she was pregnant for the second time. Gus made the best arrangements he could for her to get help during her pregnancy while he was gone during the winter and spring logging season. Come spring, he was back home on the farm and never too far away.

In the month of June their second child, a son, was born. Gus finally had a boy. He immediately dubbed him John Henry. The proud father now had two children to brag about. Gus felt that he had a real family now. The two children added a dimension to his life he had never known before, and he was more determined than ever that his children should have the best he could provide.

Not more than a week after John was born, the telegraph wires began to sing with news of Europe. Even the Baxley Banner ran a story. It seemed that Archduke Francis Ferdinand, heir to the thrones of Austria and Hungary, had been slain by a rebel group in Sarajevo, Bosnia, and Austria-Hungary had declared war on Serbia where the rebels originated.

War talk was common, even in the small towns of South Georgia, as people speculated about the war in Europe. One concern for the loggers was their timber market. Much of the timber delivered to Darien was shipped to European markets. Some old-timers remembered the Northern blockade of Southern ports during the Civil War and felt that some of the ports might be blockaded, closing some markets for their products.

President Woodrow Wilson assured the American people that the United States would remain neutral, in fact, as well as in name. Consequently, most Americans thought the war would have little or no impact on them. After all, Europe was a world away, and what happened there was not likely to affect them, especially in rural South Georgia.

Contrary to fear of closing markets, the timber demand began to rise, causing some farmers to hurry their harvest so they could return to the swamps to cut timber for the rising market. Gus was in a better position than most. He was really a part-time farmer anyway. Leaving home with the understanding that Alonzo would see that the balance of his crop was gathered, he set off to the swamps early that year.

Homer Youmans usually harvested just enough trees to help finance his farming habit, but this season he sensed an opportunity to make a killing in the timber business. Early in the fall, his crew began to fell trees for market. Homer recruited Gus to deliver his timber. He knew Gus had the expertise to deliver a raft to Darien in record time, and time was of the essence in the marketing business.

Eva and Gus talked as he prepared to leave. "I'll see you and the young'uns real often," Gus said, as he tied the straps on his pack. "I'll probably make a run about ever four days if the weather holds, and I'll come by every trip. Ain't nothin' gonna keep me from home long at the time."

"Gus, be careful. I know this is a good time to make some extra money, but I'd rather have you than all the money in the world."

Gus reached for her and held her close. "I'm always careful. Don't fret. I love you and our babies, and I plan to be around for a long time. You're gonna have a hard time gettin' rid of me, Girl," he grinned as he squeezed her.

Eva watched him leave with reservations but she knew she could never hold him. His mistress, the river, was calling and he would answer the call as long as he could put one foot in front of another.

Homer's crew, the largest he had ever employed, began to fell trees at a record pace. His goal was to cut and deliver a raft every four days, an ambitious undertaking. In order to accomplish this feat, he offered his men extra pay. This would be the best pay Gus had ever received for his work.

True to his word, Gus was home on a regular basis, although he wasn't able to make deliveries as rapidly as he would have liked. There was always the changing weather to contend with, as well as other unforeseen events. He didn't like it, but the hurry up schedule caused him to have to run at night. Ordinarily, he avoided running at night because of the added danger to his crew. A number of men had lost their lives due to accidents while running in the dark.

Any delay in Gus's return gave Eva cause for concern. She would watch the road looking for him on the day she expected his arrival. Her trepidation increased the later the hour. Sometimes she was rewarded with sight of him, as he made his way along the road. Other times, the anxiety simply built until he was finally home.

* * *

The month of December came and the rains began to fall.

Normally, the loggers would have taken a break during the rainy weather, but the urgency to make money, while it was to be had, kept them working. Any rain, except a torrential one, was ignored as they carved the trees from the banks of the river and creeks.

Gus and his companions on the raft also pushed ahead with vigor as they attempted to deliver the timbers as fast as they could be harvested. Running day and night, rain or shine, they made deliveries in record time. Gus's time at home got shorter and shorter as the pace increased.

Christmas was coming. Eva had made preparations with food and other special things for the holiday. Gus had promised her he would take a break and spend some extra time with her and the children. Eva had prepared a special homecoming for Gus and anticipated his return with more than the usual concern.

Four days had passed since Gus left with a raft. Ordinarily, he would have been home late in the day or the next day. When he failed to arrive on the fifth day, Eva became overly concerned. She expressed her worry to Susie. "I'm so worried about Gus. It's not like him to be gone this long."

Susie looked at Eva compassionately and said, "I know how you feel. Ever since Gus first started workin' the river, I've worried about him bein' out there. But he's a grown man now, and I can't tell him what to do."

"I've tried to talk to him, but he's obsessed with working timber. It's his whole life, or it seems that way sometimes."

Susie laid her hand on Eva's, "I reckon all we can do is pray that everything's okay."

"I've gotten plenty of practice prayin' these last few weeks. I know Gus's breakin' his own rule by runnin' at night, and that just makes me more concerned."

"Concerned about what, daughter?" Alonzo asked as he entered the room carrying a turn of stove wood.

"About Gus, Pa."

"Aw, he's all right. I'd guess he might have had a bit of trouble, but that don't necessarily mean anything's wrong."

"I hope you're right," Eva said, with resignation in her voice.

"Sure, I am," Alonzo said, with more conviction than he felt. He would never admit it to the women, but he was more concerned than usual. "No news is good news, remember?"

When Gus failed to return on the sixth day, Eva was beside herself with worry. She decided to try and find out what was causing the delay. Carrying John in her arms and leading Lorene by the hand, she went to see Alonzo. She found him busy under the barn shelter mending some harness.

"Pa, I'm real worried about Gus. Do you think you could help me find out if he's all right?"

Alonzo laid aside his work and turned to face Eva. "To tell you the truth, I've been wondering what's up. It ain't like Gus to be gone this long without sending word."

Eva released Lorene's hand and let her climb on the wagon. "Is there any way you could get some news?"

Alonzo scratched his beard and thought for a moment. "Homer might know something. I could maybe send one of the boys to see if he's heard anything."

"I'd really appreciate it. I can't stand not knowin' what's happened."

"Why don't you and the young'uns go on in the house? I'll round up Tom and send him to Homer's this afternoon. He ought to be back before sundown, if he takes Gus's horse."

"I really appreciate it. Come on, Lorene, let's go," she said, as she helped her down off the wagon.

* * *

Tom saddled Socks and left presently for Homer's farm. He arrived about the middle of the afternoon. Luckily, he found Homer at home taking care of some business before heading back to the swamp.

"Uncle Homer, Pa sent me to see if you had any word from Gus. He's been gone kinda long, and Eva's powerful worried about him."

Homer stacked the papers he had been working with on the corner of his desk. "No, son. I'm sorry, but I ain't got no word from Gus either. He was a day late leavin' with the raft, but he shoulda been back by now."

"Is there any way you can get some word? Pa's awful worried, and Eva's beside herself."

"I could send a telegram to the mill at Darien. They might be able to tell us if he made it there all right."

Homer reached for a sheet of paper and wrote a message, handed it to Tom, and reached in his pocket. He handed Tom a dollar and said, "Here, son. Can you take care of this for me?"

Tom took the money and message. "Yes, sir. I'll be glad to."

Dark had fallen before Tom returned, but he made it home shortly thereafter. He found the family in the kitchen where they had gathered for the evening meal. "Pa, Uncle Homer said he didn't have no news about Gus, but he give me a message and a dollar to send a telegram to the mill at Darien."

Alonzo read the message and handed it back to Tom. "That's a good idea. You wait till first light in the morning and go to town and send that telegram."

* * *

The winter dawn was breaking as Tom saddled Socks and left for town. He found the telegrapher, who had been on duty all night, nodding at his desk. "My Uncle Homer says to send this right away. I'll wait here for a reply."

The telegrapher wiped his eyes with the back of his hand, read the message, yawned, and began to tap the telegraph key. "It'll take awhile afore we get an answer. You can come back in an hour or so if you're amind."

"I'll just wait here, if it's all right."

"Suit yourself."

Tom found a seat in the depot and settled down to rest. After what seemed an eternity, the telegraph began to click, but it wasn't his message. The day telegrapher was on duty now. He listened to the clicking of the key and wrote the message.

"I'll be damned," he muttered to himself.

"What's up?" Tom asked jumping up.

"Oh, who're you?"

"I'm Tom Reynolds. I'm waiting for a telegram from Darien."

"Sorry to disappoint you, but that one was a railroad message. Seems the train was late gettin' to Jesup, and they found it derailed about half way to Brunswick."

"That might be important!" Tom exclaimed. "My brother's overdue gettin' home, and I was sent to try and get in touch by the telegraph. Was anybody hurt in the wreck?"

The telegraph key began to click again. The message ended and the telegrapher wrote it down. "You Homer Youmans' boy?"

"No. I'm Tom Reynolds. But Uncle Homer sent me to get the message."

"Oh, I forgot. Here's your message."

Tom looked at the message. It read: Gus arrived two days ago Stop.

Tom looked at the telegrapher. "Well, I know he made it to Darien all right. Question is, where's he now? Was anybody hurt in that wreck?"

"Let me see if I can find out," the telegrapher said, as he began to click the key.

"I ought to tell you, I ain't got no money to pay you for this."

"Don't worry. This one's on the house. I'm curious about this myself."

After anxious minutes, the telegraph began to click. "This is our answer," the telegrapher said, as he recorded the message. "There were two people hurt. One of them was taken to the hospital in Jesup. That's all they know."

"Thanks. You've been lots of help," Tom said, as he exited the room.

"Don't mention it. Wish I could've been more helpful."

* * *

Eva had not slept well for several nights now. Her eyes were puffy, and she had almost no energy. When she tired enough to doze off for a few minutes, she dreamed about Gus. In her dream, Gus was trying to get to her as he climbed out of a well, but he kept slipping back, and she could never quite reach his hand. She would awake with a start at any sound and lie there listening. But each time she was disappointed. It might be the wind in the trees, or some animal scampering about on the roof of the house. The daylight hours were not as difficult. She had Lorene and John to see about, and it was a comfort just to have them around.

Tom had brought news that Gus had arrived at the mill in Darien, but that was little comfort to Eva. She still did not know about the train derailment. Alonzo had thought it better not to worry her needlessly. Christmas Eve dawned, and there was still no word about Gus.

Eva had practically moved in with Alonzo and Susie. She arose and went to the kitchen to help prepare breakfast. This day wasn't going to be joyful for her. She helped Susie with the meal and washed the dishes afterward. Then she made herself busy with the children doing little things to try and keep her mind off her troubles.

Noon came and went. Eva returned to her house to tidy up. After all, she wanted things to look nice when Gus did get home. She brushed the curtains, swept the house thoroughly from ceiling to floor, and put fresh linens on the beds and tables. When she had done as much cleaning as she could find or make up, she decided to prepare for the children's Christmas. She hung stockings for Lorene and John, then on impulse she decided to hang one for Gus and one for herself. Gus would like that. He was always hiding some little trinket or other for her around Christmas.

As she placed the stocking on the mantlepiece, she breathed a prayer. "Please, Lord, let Gus come home. You know how much me and the children need him. I don't know if he's hurt or not, just let him come home, and I'll take care of him. Amen."

Eva returned to the big house to see about the children. Susie had agreed to keep them for her while she cleaned house. John was taking a nap, and Lorene played contentedly on the kitchen floor as Susie prepared the evening meal. Eva almost took them and went home, but Susie wouldn't hear of it.

"Daughter, it don't make no sense for you to go back up there and worry yourself sick waitin' for Gus. If you're not there when he gets there, he'll just truck on down here to find you. You know that. Now set yourself down and have some supper, and just stay the night."

Eva decided not to argue. After supper, the family sat around the fire and talked of Christmases past and other things. Much of the conversation was intended to distract all of them from the subject that was foremost on their minds. The family usually retired early, but this was a special night, so they sat up longer than usual. Eva was glad for the company. She knew that she wouldn't be able to sleep if she went to bed.

About ten o'clock, there was a knock at the door. That couldn't be Gus, he'd walk right in, Eva thought.

It was Homer. "I just dropped by to see if you'd heard anything else from Gus."

"Not another word," Alonzo answered.

"I just come from town, and I couldn't find any trace of him either. The trains still ain't runnin'."

Oh no, Alonzo thought. You've let the cat out of the bag now.

Eva interrupted, "What do you mean? The trains ain't runnin'!"

Homer looked like the cat that swallowed the canary and said, "I'm sorry, but there was a train wreck, and the trains from Brunswick ain't been able to get through for the past two days." He made no reference to the fact that this was prior knowledge for others.

Eva sank into her chair, placed her hands over her face and whispered, "Oh, my God." She turned pale as a ghost and sat stone still.

Susie rose and went to her side. "Now, daughter, we don't know that Gus is hurt." She didn't express her fear that he might be dead.

Tears fell from Eva's eyes as she said, "I know, but it's so hard not knowin' whether he's all right. He could be layin' somewhere needin' me, and I can't get to him to help."

Homer excused himself and went out with Alonzo following him. When they were on the front porch and out of earshot, he said, "I'm sorry. I didn't know that you hadn't told her."

"It's okay, but I'm glad you didn't let her know I was keepin' it to myself. Me and Tom is the only ones that knowed. I didn't even tell Susie."

"Look, I need to be gettin' on home. If you don't hear something by morning, send Tom to let me know, and I'll go to Jesup and look for him myself. I feel kinda responsible."

"I appreciate that, Homer. I'll let you know if he don't turn up."

Back inside, Alonzo decided to change the pace a bit. "Let's all gather around and read the Bible." He retrieved his Bible from the mantle and opened it to the book of Luke. He read Luke's account of the birth of Jesus, and then said, "Why don't we have a word of prayer? Everybody pray silent for a spell, and then I'll say a prayer for all of us."

All heads were bowed, and Eva was praying silently for Gus and his return. Finally, Alonzo began to pray, "Lord, you know what our burden is tonight, and you know how our hearts are breakin' cause we don't know where Gus is. We ask you to comfort us in this hour of need and help Gus to come home safe and sound, if it's your will, Lord. Amen."

It must have been midnight or later when a sound on the front porch caused everybody to stir. Heavy boots walked to the door and the hall door swung back. Eva heard the sounds, but she had been disappointed once tonight, so she wasn't too eager this time.

"Anybody awake?" a familiar voice called.

Eva thought she had fallen asleep and was dreaming. She could have sworn she heard Gus's voice, but that was impossible, Gus wasn't here. She sat up in her chair and caught her breath. Then, almost without realizing it, she was out of the chair headed for the front door.

Standing there in front of her was a tall man with a growth of beard, a black hat, and a stained coat. She flung herself into his arms as he lifted her and swung her off her feet hugging her to him with a grip like a grizzly bear. Eva was laughing and crying at the same time. "Gus! Gus!" She exclaimed over and over again. She thought she had to be dreaming, but if this was a dream, she didn't want to wake up.

Finally, Gus released his grip on her and put her on her feet. Susie and Alonzo were standing behind Eva watching. Gus pulled Eva under one arm and reached for his mother with the other. "It's great to see you, Ma."

Susie was usually hesitant to show affection, but she hugged him and stepped back. Alonzo reached for his hand, but, perhaps for the first time in his life since he was a small boy, hugged him.

Alonzo found his voice, "Why don't we all go to the fire? I'll put another log on, and we can talk."

The fire glowed, then rose, as tongues of flame reached the fresh wood. The room had a warm glow, but all of it wasn't from the fire.

Alonzo spoke for everybody when he said, "What happened, son? We've been worried sick for you."

"Well, to start, we were a day late leavin' with the raft. Then when we got to Darien everything seemed all right. Then the boat was late, and we missed our train in Brunswick. The next train out wasn't till mornin', and when we got about halfway to Jesup we found a derailed train. We tried to help clear the tracks, but there wasn't much we could do. The railroad was goin' to bring in special equipment to do the job so we left for Jesup on foot. We've been walking ever step of the way, except when we could hitch a ride."

"That means you've been hiking at least fifty miles," Alonzo estimated.

"Somethin' like that. And, boy, am I beat."

"Why don't you go to bed and get some rest? We'll talk some more in the mornin'."

Gus and Eva went to his old bedroom and entered quietly. They tip-toed to the bed where John and Lorene lay sleeping. Then turned to their own bed. "I really need to sleep on the floor.

I'm too dirty to sleep in a clean bed," Gus said, as he removed his clothing.

"There's no way you're gonna sleep anywhere but in this bed with me, you big hunk. I don't care how dirty you are or how much you smell. Sheets can be washed, you know."

Gus and Eva went to bed. She snuggled up to him and held on as if she would never let go. Gus was snoring soon after his head hit the pillow. Eva thought it was the most beautiful sound she had ever heard. Shortly, she fell asleep in his arms. Tonight, she didn't dream.

Chapter 13
The Fight

Gus and Eva went to their home the next morning. Gus wanted to freshen up, and Eva wanted to be with him every minute possible. When they arrived, with Gus carrying Lorene on his shoulders--this was her favorite place to ride--and Eva carrying John in her arms, Gus had a surprise for them.

"Let's see if old Saint Nick brought anything," he said, as he lowered Lorene to the floor in front of the fire place.

Eva had learned to expect almost anything from this man, so she wasn't surprised when there was actually something in each stocking for the children. A small doll filled most of Lorene's stocking. John's had a small toy hammer.

Lorene hugged her dolly with delight and said, "Thank you."

Eva looked at the toy hammer and said, "Gus, I'm not sure he can handle that."

"Don't worry; he'll grow into it."

Eva turned away to do something. "Aren't you goin' to look in yours?" Gus asked quietly.

Eva took the stocking from the mantlepiece and shook it to remove the contents. A piece of cloth fell from it and landed in her waiting hand. "Oh, it's beautiful."

Gus reached for it and said, "Let's see how it looks."

He wrapped the scarf around her shoulders, tied a knot and stepped back to admire her. "There, now. How about that?"

Eva hugged him and didn't say a word. He held her and said, "The other one wouldn't fit in the stocking. It's over on your chair."

Eva turned to look at the cloth laying in the chair. "I figure there's just about enough to make a dress, and it ought to go with the scarf," Gus whispered.

Eva held on to him. "I just don't know what I'm goin' to do with you. You slipped in here and filled those stockin's before you came to your Pa's last night, didn't you?"

Gus grinned, "Naw, I told you Saint Nick brought this stuff."

"You brought me the only present I wanted when you walked through that door."

* * *

Gus and Eva joined the Reynolds family as they celebrated together. For them, it was more a celebration of Gus's safe return than anything. They enjoyed the family reunion, but each was glad when they could leave the others behind and be by themselves.

Gus stayed home for longer than he had planned, but he felt he needed to make up for some of his time away from his family. Besides, Eva needed to see her family, and it had been some time since they had made the trip.

Bill and Annie greeted them warmly and wanted to hear all the news since their last visit. They complimented Lorene on how much she had grown and "oowed" and "aahed" over John. The visit was very pleasant, and the family talked about Gus's adventure on his last journey to Darien. Talk turned to the war in Europe, and whether or not the United States would enter the war. Bill was of the opinion that this country should stay out of the war. After all, it really didn't concern us. Gus didn't argue, but he wasn't so sure the country could stay out of the conflict which was spreading all over Europe and starting to affect American shipping.

Eva and Gus returned home, and Eva knew it was inevitable that Gus would return to the river. He did, and worked a longer season than usual. As the waters of the river began to fall in the late spring and rafting began to become more difficult, Gus returned to the farm. He had had a good winter and saved some money.

Gus planted his crop and harvested it. Prices were higher this year as merchants and bankers speculated that the war would make farm commodities more valuable. Food was exported to European countries in greater and greater quantities, as the war made it almost impossible for farmers in Europe to feed their own nations. Other exports rose as the demand had to be met from sources outside the continent.

Timber sales continued strong during the winter logging season. Gus had all the work he could do to keep the rafts moving down river. Times had never been better for the farmer and the timber industry. Land owners, particularly those with huge tracts of swamp land, were making money like they never had before. Gus even considered buying a tract and hiring a crew to harvest the timber, but decided there were too many headaches involved. Besides, he wouldn't be able to run the river, which was his favorite part of the logging business.

The logging season closed because of low water, and Gus went home to the farm again. During May of that year, Eva learned she was pregnant again. Lorene was four, and John was almost two, so at least they were old enough that she wouldn't have two babies to tend. She worked most of the summer in the fields, but had to leave off her field work as fall approached.

The harvest was almost finished, and Gus was preparing to return to the river, when Eva went into labor and delivered a boy. Gus named him Gilbert Joe; he would be called Joe. Eva now had more responsibilities with three children. To make matters worse, Joe was more sickly than Lorene or John had been. This caused her more aggravation than she had previously known. She spent long hours at night holding the baby and simply rocking him.

Gus helped all he could, but farming was a seasonal job and he had to return to logging to meet his family's needs. Once again, Eva found herself alone with their children while Gus made their living on the river. There was a plus to this experience though. Even as Eva went through those times, she was being prepared for the future in a way that she would never have understood. She was becoming a stronger person and learning what it took to survive.

* * *

The war in Europe took on new urgency. There was talk that the United States would enter the war after all. The Germans had torpedoed the *Lusitania* in 1915, but President Wilson and Congress had not declared war, even though 128 Americans were killed in the attack. Congress had voted to increase the size of the military in the summer of 1916. Early in 1917, the British intercepted a message from the Germans trying to enlist the aid of Mexico. In return, they would help Mexico recover some lands ceded to the United States by earlier treaties.

The sinking of several United States merchant ships by German submarines in the winter of 1917 sealed the fate of the United States. No longer could Americans ignore the war in Europe. In April, President Wilson delivered a declaration of war to Congress, and on the sixth day of the month, Congress ratified it.

The economy of the United States runs on war, sad, but true, at least in the twentieth century. The country now rose to a fever pitch to win the war. Congress enacted a draft requiring men from 21 to 30 years of age to register for military service. Gus was over-age, but two of his brothers were called up and served. War bonds were sold. Slogans such as "Food will win the war" and "Uncle Sam wants you" were coined and emblazoned on billboards across the country.

The government nationalized the railroads under a Rail Administration; a Fuel Administration controlled civilian use of gasoline and other fuels; and a War Trade Board controlled exports and imports.

Young men who had not been called up for military service left their homes on the farm and in small towns to work in shipyards and other related defense industries. This exodus left much of the farming to be done by the women and older men. The need for farm commodities was higher than ever, but there was money to be made in the cities, so people picked up and went where the monied jobs were.

* * *

Gus's brothers, Sam, who was just under the upper age limit, and Tom, who had reached the lower draft age, were drafted and were scheduled to leave in late spring. The family went to Baxley to see them off on the train.

War tends to bring a type of insane bravado to men, especially young men. There was lots of loud talk and bragging about how they were going to kick Kaiser Wilhelm's butt and drive them Germans back to their hovels. Excitement reigned as the train arrived and the soldiers prepared to board.

Gus, Eva, Susie, and Alonzo were standing with Tom and Sam. Susie's mood wasn't quite as jovial as some of the others around her. She was thinking that her sons might not come home as conquering heroes, but in caskets to be buried, or worse yet, be lost on some foreign battlefield, and their bodies never found. "Tom, Sam, you boys take care of yourselves, and write us. I'll be looking for letters from both of you right regular."

Tom hugged her and said, "Don't worry, Ma. I'll be real careful, and I'll let you know what's happenin'."

Sam took his turn. "Ma, you take care of yourself, and I'll keep in touch."

Alonzo cleared his throat. "Boys, you all know that I wish you well, but I want to remind you that war ain't no picnic. You're gonna see things you'll regret the rest of your life. You'll be scarred by what you see and experience, even if you survive this madness. I pray that you'll come through this alive, but I know you might not. Whatever happens, your Ma and I love you and want the best for you. It'd be best if you didn't have to go, but since you ain't got much choice, stand up and make us proud."

This speech sobered Tom and Sam, especially Tom. He took his father's hand, then caught him in his arms, hugged him, and said with feeling, "I will, Pa."

Sam hugged Alonzo and said, "We'll give a good account of these Reynolds' boys, Pa. Don't you worry."

Gus shook hands with each of his brothers in turn. "Tom, little brother, take care of yourself and don't let none of them foreign gals capture you and keep you."

"Aw, heck, Gus, you know me."

"Yeah, that's what worries me."

Sam took his brother's hand as Gus said. "I'll look after Ma and Pa. Thanks for all the help you've been."

"Thanks," Sam grinned.

The conductor called, "All aboarddd," and the men began to file on to the coaches. The loading took several minutes, and the engineer gave a blast on the whistle just to remind any stragglers that he was about to pull out. Finally, the train started to move as the drive wheels ground into the sand dropped on the track to give them traction. As the train moved out, men were waving to their families and sweethearts. The waves were returned, but the enthusiasm wasn't quite as high as it had been.

* * *

With Tom and Sam gone, other family members had to assume their chores and take up the slack left by their absence. Gus took on more farm work than he had done for some years now. Farmers usually worked from sunup to sundown, but he found himself working after night. During harvest that fall, many a sheet of cotton or pile of corn was loaded by the light of the moon. He seldom left the woods or the fields before dark.

Joe was improving. Eva didn't have to spend as much time caring for him. She helped out in the fields when she could. Lorene was five now and growing into quite a little lady. She could help in the kitchen and was assigned chores appropriate to her abilities. If there was one thing Eva and Gus both agreed with on the subject of child rearing, it was that children should be taught to work.

John turned three that summer, and Lorene also made a pretty good babysitter in a pinch. She would spend hours entertaining her little brothers. Sometimes it was necessary to carry the children to the fields. They would play in the shade of a tree while their parents hoed or plowed or harvested the crops.

Gus began to bond with John. He held him and talked to him

and took him along when he could on short errands. Gus felt he was really living with a capital "L" as some would have said. His family had always been important to him, but now he felt as if he were wealthy, although he didn't have a lot of money. It seemed he recalled that somewhere in the Bible it said, "Children are like arrows. Blessed is the man whose quiver is full of them."

* * *

News of the war came regularly by way of city newspapers delivered as much as a week late. Letters were rare, but occasionally Susie would hear from either Sam or Tom. As the time dragged on, the mail came less and less. The last letter from Tom told them he was somewhere in France.

The timber market was still good, although exports were not as high as they had been. Domestic sales were up as a result of the national frenzy to build ships faster than the German U-Boats could sink them. Ships were built mostly of metal, but wood, especially hardwood, was in demand.

Once again, the loggers were ahead with their work as they anticipated the new market for their product. Piles of logs were lying on river banks just waiting to be shipped to their destination. The mill at Doctor Town was now buying more hardwoods and shipping them to domestic customers. This made it easier to deliver since a trip to Doctor Town took at least two days less than one to Darien.

Gus had all the work he could handle and made regular runs on the river, averaging about three trips every two weeks. The frequency of the trips meant that riding the train home was no longer an option. He and his crew became a familiar sight in the Jesup depot. The ticket agents and conductors knew them on sight, if not by name.

* * *

On one occasion, Gus and his crew had made a delivery to Doctor Town and were waiting for their train. The depot was crowded with people trying to get home to see their families or get back to their work in the city. Or crowded with new recruits headed for basic training. As a result of the nationalization of the railroad, there was almost always a military presence anywhere along the railroads.

A sergeant who was in charge of a small group of men was blustering about, giving orders to everybody, civilians included. He really had no authority over the civilians, but this man was the type who let his uniform go to his head. There are some people that simply cannot be given any vestige of authority. Give them a uniform, badge, or title, and immediately, they magnify their own importance to the point of becoming obnoxious to everyone around. More than one hotheaded, self-important fool has found himself in dire straits as a result of his ego.

Gus didn't hunt trouble, but those who knew him knew he didn't walk away from it either. So far, he had ignored the loud-mouthed sergeant and probably would have continued to do so if the soldier had not continued to aggravate the situation. The second time the sergeant pushed him as he went by was the last straw.

"Hey, you! Get out of my way," the sergeant yelled.

"You talkin' to me?" Gus asked quietly.

"You damn right I am. Army's got jurisdiction here, and we don't need no damn civilians in our way."

Gus looked him straight in the eye and said evenly, "That don't give you the right to push folks around."

"What the hell do you know? You damn dumb cracker."

"I know if you push me one more time, you're gonna regret it."

"Well, I'll be damned. Boys, we got a tough one here. Look at this bunch. Ain't had a bath in a week. Smell to high heaven. Damn ignorant civilians. They gonna show us army boys up?"

"No, sir," a chorus of voices answered.

Gus and his crew stood together, as the crowd moved away from what was clearly an explosive situation. The band of soldiers faced the rafters and were prepared to fight if their sergeant gave the word.

Gus spoke quietly and evenly. "As near as I can tell, Sergeant, it's your education that needs fixin'. If you'll just step outside I'll see what I can do to remedy that."

"Okay, men, just stand away. This cracker's gonna educate me. Cracker, don't you know you're talkin' to a United States Army Officer?" he asked as he laid his swagger stick across his shoulder.

"You could've fooled me," Gus said, watching his eyes for any sign of action.

"You damn stupid cracker, we'll settle this right here," he spat as he brought the swagger stick through a curve intended for the side of Gus's head.

Gus saw the blow coming and warded it off with his left hand grasping the sergeant's wrist and twisting it until the stick fell from his hand. The sergeant was surprised, to say the least, but he regrouped and drove a left into Gus's middle. He got quite a surprise there, too. It felt like hitting a wall. Hanging on to the sergeant's right arm, Gus attempted to twist it into a hammer lock, but the sergeant gave with the twist and freed himself from Gus's hold.

Completing a circle, the sergeant was able to connect with Gus's chin, temporarily putting him off balance. The sergeant followed through with a lunge that took them both to the floor. As they wrestled on the floor, Gus brought his knee between the sergeant's legs and kneed him in the groin. Groaning in pain, the sergeant rolled over and lay still, clutching himself.

Gus stood waiting as the sergeant rose to his feet still groaning. "You stupid son-of-bitch. I'm gonna kill you," the sergeant shouted as he charged. He made the same mistake so many others had. He charged furiously without thinking of the possible result. Gus side-stepped the charge and clipped him behind the head with a rabbit punch. He fell like a sack of potatoes and lay still.

Gus stood still, gulping air into his lungs. He felt the spot on his chin where he had been hit. It was starting to swell. Everybody was standing still as if in a dream. Gus moved to retrieve his hat from the floor. Stooping down, he picked it up, straightened the crown, and placed it on his head.

One of the soldiers was kneeling by the sergeant. "Sarge! Get up, Sarge! You ain't gonna let that cracker get the best of you, are you?" The sergeant didn't respond.

The sound of a police whistle broke the silence that followed. "What's goin' on here?" a tall, burly police officer asked.

"This cracker here has hurt the Sarge real bad," the soldier kneeling by the sergeant answered.

The police officer knelt by the fallen man and felt his carotid artery. "Somebody, get a doctor!" he commanded.

The policeman rose to his feet,"Did anybody see what happened?"

It wasn't exactly a bright question. There were a roomful of witnesses. Gus didn't volunteer any information. One soldier decided to take the offensive. "This cracker picked a fight with the Sarge," he said, pointing at Gus.

The policeman looked at Gus, "How about it?"

Gus looked the policeman in the eye and said, "I'd say it was the other way 'round."

"That's right," a voice from the crowd agreed.

A man carrying a medical bag came through the crowd. "Let me through here, please. I'm a doctor."

The crowd parted, and the doctor knelt by the man on the floor. He checked the pulse at first one point and then another. His hands worked up and down the spine and lingered at the base of the skull. Taking a scalpel from his bag, he placed it over the man's nose. There wasn't any sign of breathing. The metal should have clouded showing moisture from the respiratory system. "This man's dead," the doctor announced matter-of-factly.

"How'd he die?" queried the policeman.

"As near as I can tell, his neck's broke."

The soldier who had knelt by the sergeant pointed an accusing finger at Gus," That son-of-bitch is a murderer."

"No, he ain't," a voice from the crowd protested.

"Who said that?" the policeman turned toward the sound of the voice.

"I did," said a short man with a balding head. "I saw the whole thing, and I'll be damned if I'm gonna stand by and see a man railroaded for standing up to that piece of trash."

"Who're you?" the policeman demanded.

"Smith. Sam Smith."

"What happened?"

"This fellow was blusterin' around, shovin' folks, and givin' orders to everybody like he was God Almighty," he said, pointing to the man on the floor. "He shoved this man at least twice before he challenged him. When this gent in the black coat called his hand, he got mad as hell and started callin' him a cracker and cussin' at him. Then the sergeant swung at him with that club over there." Smith pointed to the stick lying on the floor where it had fallen.

The policeman turned to Gus. "What's your name?" he asked.

"Gus Reynolds," Gus answered quietly.

"Well, Mister Reynolds, we're gonna have to have you stick around for a coroner's hearing, but if we can confirm Mister Smith's story, it looks like self-defense to me."

"Okay," Gus answered. "I'll be here. When do I have to appear?"

"Ain't no reason it can't be done tomorrow. Meanwhile though, I got to have some bond. Just so's you don't change your mind and skip out on me."

"How much?"

"I can't say for sure. That'll be up to the chief down at the calaboose."

Smith spoke up, "I'll stand good for the bond."

"That won't be necessary," Gus responded.

"It'll be my pleasure."

Gus accompanied the policeman to the city police department. His companions, along with Smith, came, too. The chief had to be summoned to hear the charges and set the bond. He wasn't any too happy about the incident, but did listen as the evidence was given by Smith once more.

"The coroner'll hear this tomorrow morning. Meanwhile, why don't you leave me one hundred dollars in bond money, and you can sleep somewhere besides our jail. It's kinda crowded lately, what with all the ruckus we've had lately with all these soldiers fightin' and fussin'."

Over Gus's protest, Smith handed a hundred dollar bill to the chief. "It's worth every penny. That S.O.B.'s been shovin' people around for weeks now, and you're the first one who's had the guts to call his hand."

Outside, Smith continued, "I reckon you boys need a place to hole up for the night. You're welcome to stay at my house."

"Why're you doin' this for me?" Gus asked.

"Like I said, I don't like the way the army's been lettin' that sergeant push folks around. It's about time we let them know we're fed up with this mess."

The coroner's inquest was scheduled next morning at nine o'clock. A few minutes before the hearing began, a well dressed man approached Gus and introduced himself. "How do you do? I'm Ben Broxton, attorney."

Gus couldn't quite understand why Broxton was there. "Pleased to make your acquaintance."

"I'm here to represent you, if you want me."

"Represent me?"

"Yeah. Sam said you might need somebody."

"Oh. Well, Sam's been a lot of help, but this is supposed to be a simple hearin', and it was self-defense."

"Mister Reynolds, take my word for it. There ain't nothin' simple when it comes to the law. Laws are made by the few to intimidate the many. Besides, there's no logic to the law and people twist it to suit themselves. I ought to know, I've been practicin' it long enough."

"You ought to know I don't have money to pay you."

"If this hearin' goes okay, you won't need it. If it don't, then we'll work something out."

The coroner's inquest was called to order in the city courtroom. "This hearin' is now in session. I remind you that the purpose of this hearin' is to determine cause and circumstance in the death of Sergeant Frank Sutton. This is not a trial. However, the evidence presented here will be used to determine if there ought to be an indictment and trial in this matter. The witnesses will confine themselves to direct testimony concerning the events that transpired last evening concerning the death of the deceased. We'll begin with Corporal Axton. Corporal, please take the stand."

Axton's testimony was naturally biased toward his sergeant claiming that he had exercised his right as an officer of the army. Other soldiers were of the same opinion, but one had the courage to speak against his fellows, causing raised eyebrows from more than one person present. It became clear that he and his sergeant had no love lost between them. The mouse was becoming a man as he took on the task of admitting that Sutton had indeed attacked Gus.

The tide of testimony had turned, and Sam Smith's clinched the point that Gus had indeed defended himself in the fight. The coroner recessed the hearing for an hour.

Broxton sat with Gus as the hearing was in recess. "It looks like there might be some justice here after all. The testimony of that soldier sure puts Sutton in a bad light."

"I hope so," Gus responded.

"We should know in a few minutes. How about a cup of coffee?" Broxton asked.

* * *

The courtroom had filled, and everybody waited for the coroner to return. Five minutes later, he seated himself at the desk, banged his gavel, and declared the hearing in order.

"The evidence given in this hearin' indicates that Sergeant Sutton died of a blow to the back of the neck. Said blow broke his neck, and he died as a result of a broke neck. The blow was delivered by Mister Reynolds after being attacked by Sergeant Sutton. I hereby rule that Sergeant Sutton died by the hand of Mister Reynolds as an act of self-defense."

Gus breathed a sigh of relief. Broxton slapped him on the back. Axton shot him a dagger with his eyes. The coroner rapped his gavel on the desk and declared, "This hearin's adjourned."

"Well, I guess you won't be needin' my services after all," Broxton said.

"Thanks," Gus returned. "How much I owe you?"

"Don't owe me nothin'. Glad to be available."

Gus decided there must be some lawyers who were not thieves. This one seemed different.

As they left the courtroom, the soldiers glared at the rafters and would have followed them down the street, except they were halted by the police officer who had investigated the incident. "You boys ain't had enough trouble for one day?" he asked. "If you take my advice, you'll let them fellows alone, or some of you might end up keeping your sergeant company down at the undertaker's."

Axton started to speak, thought better of it, and walked off in the opposite direction followed by his fellow soldiers. The policeman watched them disappear around a corner and said to himself, "That's the smartest thing you boys done recently. I ain't too sure I'd want to tangle with a man who just killed somebody with his bare hands."

Deep in his gut, Gus was struggling with what had happened. He wasn't happy that he'd had to kill a man, but it wasn't an option under the circumstances. Either you defended yourself or you let him kill you. The second choice didn't seem the better one.

Chapter 14

The Car

The war news was more encouraging now. The Allies were advancing against the Germans and the Central Powers. Americans had taken up positions in France and other places, and, for the first time, it seemed the enemy might soon be defeated.

Letters from Tom and Sam were rare. When they managed to get messages home, there wasn't much news in them. Their family took comfort from knowing that at least they had been able to write a few words.

At home, the war effort was now in full swing. Demand for farm products were at an all-time high, timber sales were still strong, and the economy was booming. This economic shot in the arm gave people money to spend that they would not have had otherwise.

Black marketeers were doing a booming business, too. It seemed that certain people always find a way to profit from other people's misery. The poor man went to the trenches, and the rich man got richer. There is no more patriotic person than the one whose pockets are stuffed with revenues in the name of defending his country.

The full impact of the war began to come home to local people as coffins began to arrive with the remains of their loved ones. There was really no way to tell if the bodies were who they were supposed to be. Caskets were sealed and were not supposed to be opened. One family insisted that their son's coffin be opened. All they found inside was a layer of earth with his dog tags lying on top. No one knows how many empty coffins were buried, with families believing they had lain their loved ones to rest.

Communities were pulled together by funerals. Mothers comforted one another, while fathers talked quietly with each other. Most of them accepted the loss with resignation, but it's hard to be patriotic when your young son's dead, and his body, if it is his body, lies in your living room. Funeral sermons were often filled with talk about patriotic service, but to a grieving parent, it was mostly rhetoric.

Hardly a day went by that Susie didn't think of Tom and Sam and breathe a prayer on their behalf. Alonzo didn't say much, but it was clear that he too was concerned for the safety of his sons.

The train arrived carrying a casket that supposedly held the remains of a neighbor's son. The local undertaker met the train and loaded the casket into his hearse. The family had been notified of the impending arrival, so the undertaker delivered the body to the family home. That evening, families came from all over the neighborhood to bring food and visit with the grieving family. The atmosphere was quiet and subdued as the family received their neighbors.

Susie met the grieving mother with outstretched arms. "Oh, Addie, I'm so sorry."

Addie nodded her head as tears welled up in her eyes, and she and Susie hugged each other. "I'm so glad you came. It's so hard to give him up."

Susie didn't know quite what to say, but a squeeze of her hand assured Addie that she was there to comfort her. They seated themselves near the coffin and talked quietly.

"He was a good boy," Addie said. "Oh, I know he was mischievous sometimes, but all boys are. It seems like it was only yesterday I was pickin' him up, kissin' his cuts and scratches to make them better. He might have been a grown man, but to me he's still my little boy. Susie, I don't know how I'm goin' to get along without him."

Meanwhile Alonzo and Bob had shook hands and seated themselves on the front porch. Bob was keeping a stiff upper lip, but he was visibly shaken by the loss of his son. "Bud," this was

Alonzo's nickname among friends, "I just don't see why our young'un's got to die in this damn war. It ain't like we was fighting for our land or anything. I reckon it sounds selfish, but I can't see givin' up my boy this way."

"Don't be too hard on yourself, Bob. If it was my boy, I think I might feel the same."

"You know what really galls me? It's them big shots that's sittin' on their butts makin' a killin' while my boy goes and gets hisself killed, and for what? Just so's they can make a dollar off'n somebody. They get rich, and I have to put my boy in the ground. I tell you, it just ain't right."

"I can't argue with that."

The funeral took place the following day with the military honor guard in attendance. After the preacher had finished his remarks at the graveside, seven riflemen, led by their sergeant, fired their weapons over the casket three times, completing a twenty-one gun salute. The guard then folded the flag that had been draped over the coffin and presented it to Addie. She took it and held it to her breast as the bugler played taps and the casket was lowered into the ground.

As the family moved away from the grave, friends stopped and spoke to them quietly. Gus and Eva were among those attending. When everyone had had a chance to speak to the family, the mourners departed. The presence of friends is almost always welcome at times like these, but there comes a time when we must go home to face the reality that our loved ones are gone. The empty place at the table, the empty bed where they slept, and other places that conjure up memories of the deceased.

* * *

On January 8, 1918, President Wilson made public his fourteen points offering the Central Powers peace and encouraging the rank and file to overthrow their governments. In March, the Russians signed a treaty with the Germans and lost territory to neighboring Central Powers. The western front had been quiet for the Germans, now they made an all-out attempt to storm the Allies in an effort to bring Great Britain to her knees.

The battle raged as the Allies retreated, and then assaulted the German lines with renewed vigor. The tide had finally turned. The Central Powers were now in retreat, and finally, on November 7, a German delegation met Allied commanders to sue for peace. The treaty called for a cessation of hostilities on the eleventh hour of the eleventh day of the eleventh month. The guns fell silent. The war was over.

The news spread as Americans celebrated and politicians echoed President Wilson's words that the world was now safe for democracy. Most families were content to know their sons would be coming home.

The train brought someone home almost every day. There were happy reunions as families and friends met their returning sons, brothers, or sweethearts at the local depot. The only thing that dampened their spirits was the memory of those who had left in a fever of glory never to return alive.

News from Tom and Sam had not been plentiful. As far as anyone knew, they were alive and well. After what seemed like an eternity, Susie received word that Tom was being mustered out and would be coming home as soon as he could arrange transportation.

Gus agreed to meet Tom as he came in. Susie wanted to prepare a special homecoming for him, and Alonzo's arthritis had laid him up for a spell, so they would see him when he got home. Another factor in the decision was the possible time of arrival. The train might not arrive until late in the night or early in the morning, depending on how you thought of it.

Tom's train was due to arrive on Wednesday and Gus waited for the train. Sure enough, he wasn't on the evening train. So Gus found himself waiting at the depot. The night was still, and the sound of rain frogs croaking punctuated the silence from time to time.

As Gus sat by himself on a bench, another person entered the waiting room and seated himself across from Gus. "Evenin'," the man said. Gus nodded, acknowledging the man's greeting.

"You waitin' for the train?" the newcomer inquired.

"Yeah."

"Me, too. My boy's supposed to come in tonight."

"My brother's due sometime today. At least, that's what his letter said. He wasn't on the evening train so, I'm waitin' for the next train."

"When's the next one due?" asked the newcomer.

"Midnight, I think."

"Well, we've got ourselves a long wait then."

"That's a fact."

Waiting can be one of the most boring tasks known to man. Most people find that they need to be busy about something, even if it's passive. Boredom overtook Gus and his waiting companion. Finally, the newcomer spoke. "I'm Clint. What's your handle?"

"Gus."

"Well, now, Gus since we know one another, how about we find us something to entertain ourselves?"

"What'd you have in mind?"

"There's a checkerboard over there by the ticket window. Why don't I see if we can have a loan of it?"

"Sounds okay to me."

Clint strolled over to talk to the ticket agent and returned with the checkerboard on a small table. Placing it between them, he poured the checkers out of a small bag. "Red or black?" he asked.

"Don't matter none to me."

"Okay, I'll take the red then. I'm the challenger so you move first."

The two men played their game, and then another. By the time the train whistle sounded they had probably played a dozen or so leisurely games. It didn't matter who won, so the competition wasn't too strong.

The train chugged into the station and came to a stop with and screech of brakes and a hiss of steam. The conductor stepped down and went to check with the ticket agent. Nobody else exited the train.

Gus and Clint stood near the door to check for their expected arrivals. "It looks like our wait ain't over," Clint observed.

"I'm afraid you're right."

"Want to play another game?"

"I don't think so. I need some sleep. I think I'll take a nap."

Gus awoke with a start. The train whistle sounded twice more as the 4 A. M. rolled into the station. Gus lay still and listened for the sound of footsteps on the platform. Sure enough, there was more than one set. Rising from his place on the depot bench, he placed his hat on his head and walked toward the door. Clint followed him. A soldier carrying a duffle bag walked through the door and called out, "Pa," when he spied Clint.

Gus was thinking, "Oh, no. Another wait," when a second soldier followed the first. "Welcome home, little brother," Gus said, extending his hand to Tom. The little part wasn't accurate. Tom was as tall as Gus and heavier. He had certainly changed since he'd left.

"Gus, you're a sight for sore eyes. You alone?"

"Yep. I hope you didn't expect a band this time of night."

"No. Really, I didn't. How's Ma and Pa?"

"They're fine. Just on pins and needles waitin' for you."

"I'm ready. Boy, it's great to be home. I can't wait to eat some of Ma's cookin' and go for a stroll in the fields and woods."

"How was Europe?" Gus asked, as Tom lifted his bag and followed him out to the waiting wagon.

"Europe was a real hell-hole. You wouldn't believe some of the things I saw."

"I expect you're right. I believe it was Sherman who said, 'War is hell,' about the time he burned Atlanta."

The brothers mounted the wagon and Gus drove out of town headed to the farm. "You seen Mabel since I left?" Tom asked.

"Can't say as I have. Why, you didn't have enough female company overseas?"

"Had plenty, but it ain't like havin' a South Georgia girl. There's somethin' special about them."

The early morning reunion that followed was warm and just what Tom needed. He didn't realize how homesick he was until he actually set foot back on the farm. The warm country breakfast topped it off.

* * *

In the spring of 1919, Eva and Gus's fourth child, a girl, was born. Eva named her Alice. Life was good. The men of the family had returned from war, and everyone was reasonably healthy. Alonzo felt that he was fortunate to have his family together again, so much, that he decided to hold a small family reunion.

The first Sunday in May was chosen for the special day, and family members were informed that they would celebrate the safe return of their soldiers. A dinner of just about any type of food anyone in the family knew how to prepare was laid out on tables in the yard. The women fussed over details, small and large, while the children frolicked, chasing one another around the yard.

Alonzo stood at the head of the table and said, "May I have your attention."

The crowd quieted, and the adults hushed the children as they gathered around the table. Alonzo waited for a moment and then continued, "This is a good day in the lives of this family. The Lord has brought our sons home safe from foreign shores. We have little ones running around under foot and newborns in our midst. We have a bountiful table of food, and all the things in the world to be thankful for. This day is blessed as we give thanks to the Lord for his many blessin's. Let's bow our heads in prayer."

Everyone helped themselves to the food and enjoyed a veritable feast. Conversations ranged from what happened in the war to farming and crops. Alice got passed around among the women and older girls. She enjoyed it for awhile, but soon tired, and Eva put her to bed for an afternoon nap.

Susie's nephew, Johnny Youmans, an amateur photographer, was present at the family reunion. He was always looking for an opportunity to practice his art and encouraged everybody to let him make their picture. He had just approached Gus on the subject.

"It don't matter that much to me," Gus said, as he finished a piece of blueberry pie, "but I'll probably break your camera."

"Aw, come on, Gus, if I can get you in the picture I'll be able to get everybody else. How about it?"

"What you want me to do?" Gus asked, as he put his plate on the dirty dish stack.

"Just get'em all gathered round so I can take the picture."

"Where you want us?"

"Over by the house. No. I think in front of the barn's better."

Gus walked out to the middle of the crowd and said in a raised voice. "I need your attention here." After a few seconds the family quieted. "Johnny here, wants to take our picture. I warned him he'd break his camera, but he still wants to try it. If you'll look real close, you'll see he's got patches on his britches. Let's let him take our picture so he can buy himself a decent pair of pants."

The women rounded up the children and scrubbed their faces until they shone. Everyone was told to comb their hair and put on their jackets. You just didn't make a photograph unless you were spruced up.

Gus accompanied Johnny to his car to get his camera. Johnny rummaged in the back seat and pulled out a late model Kodak and tripod. Gus stood admiring the car. "That's a Ford, ain't it?" he asked.

"Yep, Henry's been buildin' 'em for some time now you know. It's a 1915 Model T."

Gus walked around the car looking at it from different angles. "If I ain't bein' too nosey, what does one like that cost?"

"A new one runs around four hundred dollars, but you might find a used one for half that price."

"That's a lot of green."

"Yep, but it's a lot faster than a horse, and it don't get tired."

"I've been thinkin' about buyin' one, but I'll have to think some more at that price."

Gus and Johnny returned to find most of the family ready for their picture. Gus helped line up family members by fathers, mothers and children. "Everybody squeeze in tight now so Johnny can get us all in at one time." He took John and Joe and stood them in front of him. Eva held Alice and Lorene stood in front of her.

Johnny placed the camera, checked the viewfinder, and moved the camera back a few steps. "Everybody hold real still now. If you wiggle, you'll blur the picture."

John just had to test this to see if it worked. He wiggled, and Gus's hand came down and held him and Joe firmly on the shoulder.

"Everybody ready?" Johnny asked. "Here we go."

The shutter clicked as he pulled the cord and captured the family for posterity. "Just one more now to be sure we've got a good one." He reset the camera and took a second shot of the same pose. This photograph became a family treasure as time passed, giving the children a glimpse of their childhood and fond memories of their parents.

* * *

Gus decided he would look for a car after all. He reasoned that he could save enough time on trips to make it worth the extra money. Besides, it would be nice to own something just because he wanted it.

Jarman's in Baxley had been selling cars on order for a some time. Gus went to see if they had any for sale.

"We just order them as folks ask us to. You know there ain't too many in the whole county. If you wanted us to order you one, we could," the salesperson advised Gus.

"I'm not sure I can buy a new one. Do you have any trade-ins?"

"We usually don't take trades, but once in a while somebody has one they'd like to sell when they buy a new one."

"Do you know anybody who's looking to buy?"

"Not right off hand."

"I'm interested. How about lettin' me know if you get one?"

"Okay, sure. I'll let you know."

Four or five weeks passed, and Gus had about given up on the idea of buying the car when word came that Jarman had an order for a new car, and the buyer would be willing to sell his older car. Gus got the name of the man and went to see him.

The house was on the edge of town. Gus knocked at the door and waited as he heard footsteps approaching the door. "Good morning, ma'am. Is Mr. Jones around? I understand he has a car he might be willing to sell."

"I think he's out back. Just walk on out there."

Gus found his way around the house where Jones was working on a mowing machine. "Howdy, I'm Gus Reynolds. They tell me down at Jarman's you've got a car you might be interested in sellin'."

Jones straightened up and stretched his arms. "These dang blades don't hold an edge worth nothin'. Say you're interested in the car, are you?"

"That's right," Gus said, leaning against the post of the shed.

"Well, I just decided I'd get me a new one. This'un I've got has kinda started to wear some, if you know what I mean."

"What kind you got?"

"It's a Model T. I ain't quite sure what year. It don't make no difference nohow. They've all looked alike since the year eight. Come on over to the barn."

Gus followed Jones to a building with a shelter on one side. The car sat under the shelter with the top folded back. The body seemed to be in good shape. Gus looked it over and asked, "Can I start her up?"

"Sure. You ever handle one of these things?"

"Not much. Drove my cousin's once."

"Here let me show you how to start it. First, you need to be sure the parkin' brake's set. This thing could run over you if you start it wrong and the brake ain't on. Now this lever sets the spark. It needs to be right about here," Jones said, pushing the handle up. "Next thing's to set your throttle like so."

Walking around to the front of the car, Jones placed the starter crank through the slot in the grill and tested the hold as the pin on the end of the crank slipped into place. "You got to be careful here, too. This thing can break a man's arm if he don't watch it." Jones turned the crank counterclockwise and pulled up on the crank. The engine sputtered and died. He set the crank again and pulled. This time the engine came to life, but sputtered. "She needs a little more spark," he said, as he moved to the steering wheel and adjusted the lever. The engine leveled off and ran smoothly.

"Want to take her for a spin?" Jones shouted over the roar of the engine.

"Sure, why not?"

Gus climbed into the driver's seat, placed his hands firmly on the wheel, and prepared to place his feet on the pedals. Jones was now in the passenger seat. "The pedal on the left is your forward gears. Push it half way down and release the brake." Gus complied with the directions. "Now press it to the floor." The car moved forward slowly. "Now give it just a little more throttle." Gus pulled the lever a bit lower. "Now, when you take your foot off the pedal you shift into high by pushin' the brake lever full ahead. Do it easy like, or you'll choke her down." Gus eased off the pedal pushing the brake lever forward at the same time. The car jerked, but the engine kept running. "Not bad. Now watch where you're goin'. This ain't no horse so it don't go around posts and such. It don't answer to 'whoa' neither."

Gus had begun to get a feel for the car and was able to miss the obvious things, but potholes were another matter. The car had solid rubber tires and bounced something awful as he hit one hole and then another. "How do you stop it?" Gus shouted.

"Pull your brake lever halfway back and apply your brakes with your right foot. Be careful and don't hit the wrong pedal. The one in the middle's reverse."

Gus pulled back on the lever and applied the brake. The car seemed to continue indefinitely, but finally came to a stop. He locked the hand brake and took his feet off the pedals. "I think I can get the hang of it," he said, as he grinned at Jones.

"Sure, you can. Ain't nothin' to it."

Gus managed to drive back to Jones's house. He stopped the car in front. "Just push the throttle all the way up. That'll kill the engine."

"How much you asking for her?" Gus asked, as he leaned back in the seat and looked at Jones.

"I was thinkin' maybe a hundred seventy-five, but she needs some work. How about a hundred fifty?"

Gus thought for a moment. "I can do that, I think. Okay, it's a deal."

Gus paid Jones in cash, and Jones wrote him a receipt. "There now. She's all yours. Hope you enjoy it," Jones said, as he handed Gus the paper.

Jones accompanied Gus out to the car to supervise his starting and to give him hints if he needed them. It took some time, but Gus mastered the cranking procedure and was on his way in a few minutes.

* * *

"Leaping Lena," as Gus called his car, was a conversation piece for some time to come. Gus enjoyed tinkering with her and it was a good thing he did. Model T's were known for their mechanical deficiencies. Among its other shortcomings were mechanical brakes, or no brakes, to which their owners often attested. Other times, try as he would, the ignition simply refused to cooperate. The engine could be started by pushing the car, so it became a common labor. So common, in fact, that John, who turned five that summer, vividly remembered it the rest of his life.

"Leaping Lena" did make trips faster than a horse, but there were also problems that were largely unknown to the horse and wagon. Mud was a common problem. Roads were not paved, and it was not unusual to find yourself stuck in the mud. Most drivers carried shovels as part of their standard equipment. Running out of gas was also a familiar occurrence. Many a car was towed with a team of horses to the nearest filling station.

Drivers were also disliked because their noisy automobiles scared horses. Most of them were cussed out more than they cared to remember.

The joy of the car was being able to make a trip to Eva's parents or simply go for a Sunday drive. These drives were usually done leisurely and slowly. Drivers who continually practiced this form of motoring were known as "Sunday Drivers."

Gus and Eva were sitting on top of the world. Some of us think we would like to know what the future holds. Others claim to be able to tell us the future, but the fact is, had Gus and Eva known the future, they would not have liked it. It is better to live in a state of hope than despair.

Chapter 15
Last Run

Life returned to normal for the Reynolds family. There was farming to be done and turpentine to work. Gus and his brothers were busy with both of these chores. The extended family was growing. Tom and Mabel married. There were four boys and all of them had wives. The grandchildren numbered more than a dozen. Life just seemed good to Alonzo and Susie. They had seldom been happier.

Lorene had turned seven in the spring, John was five in the summer, and Joe would be three in October. Gus delighted in his children and spent time with them when he could. John especially had his father's attention. Gus took him with him more now than ever. Some of John's fondest memories were of riding with his father in "Leaping Lena."

Times were still good economically, but the height of prosperity seemed to have passed, at least for awhile. Crops didn't sell quite as well in the fall as they had a year ago. The country was winding down from the boom brought on by the war. Demand for timber, however, continued as new building projects began in the country.

Locally, a road bridge was being constructed between Appling and Tattnall Counties. This was the first such structure across the Altamaha River named in honor of Mills B. Lane, who was the major stockholder in the company constructing the bridge.

Foreign markets were still open. With the reconstruction in post-war Europe, the demand was almost as high as ever. The market at Darien was good and local landowners tried to sell their timber where prices were best.

Gus went back to the river early in the fall, but found time to spend with his family. He would turn thirty-nine in November, and Eva had planned a special celebration for his birthday. The trick was to get him home for the occasion. It wasn't easy. Gus didn't think too much about birthdays. It wasn't that he objected to growing older, he just didn't attach much importance to their celebration.

The big day arrived, and Gus was home, by some minor miracle. Eva had invited members of the Reynolds clan, who were nearby, to join in the celebration. Gus wasn't an old man by anyone's reckoning, but he had turned almost completely gray. He took a lot of teasing about his hair.

"Brother, I declare you're almost completely covered with snow," Tom teased him.

"That's okay, just because there's snow on the roof don't mean the fire's gone out in the furnace," Gus joked.

"We gonna have to get you a walkin' cane."

"Not for a while, I hope."

The evening meal was served and everyone enjoyed themselves. The conversation was ambling along going nowhere in particular when John, who was standing at the kitchen window, called out, "Pa, come see the rabbits."

Gus went to the window and looked out into the night. "Where John?"

"Right there. In the lamp light."

"I don't see anything, son."

"I see them. There they are. White rabbits playin' in the light."

Gus looked again. "Son, I don't see a thing."

"They're there, Pa, just as plain as day."

Eva had picked up on the conversation. "John, are you playing that game again?" she asked.

"What do you mean?" Gus asked, turning to Eva.

"He keeps tellin' us he sees rabbits out there almost every night lately, but I don't see a thing."

"How long's this been goin' on?" Gus asked.

"For about a week," Eva replied.

Gus reached down and picked up John. He carried him out the kitchen door and into the yard. Standing near the house, he looked at the pattern of light on the ground cast from the kitchen lamp. "Where do you see the rabbits, John?"

"I don't see them now, Pa. I only see them when I'm standing at the window."

Gus considered the situation for a moment, then he said, "John, I know that little boys have a good imagination sometimes. I used to make up imaginary things when I was a boy. Now, I think you're carryin' this thing a little too far. Your Ma's upset by what you're sayin'. It's okay to imagine things, but I don't want you talkin' about this anymore. Especially around your Ma. Do you understand?"

"But, Pa, I saw them."

"Look, John, I'm gonna spank you if you don't stop."

"Yes, sir, I won't tell Ma about it no more."

"Okay, that's good. Now let's go get another piece of that delicious cake your Ma baked."

Later that night when Gus and Eva were alone, they talked. "I had a talk with John about his imagination," Gus told her.

"Good. I don't understand it. He's been carryin' on like that for some time. It worries me."

Gus reached for her and held her close, "I don't think it's anything serious. He's just imaginin' it. He's a normal little boy, and he sees things in the dark. I was afraid of the dark when I was a child."

Eva hugged him and said, "I hope you're right."

* * *

Christmas came and Gus did his best to make it special for each of the children. He bought Eva a new washtub and filled the bottom with fruit and candy for the family. Each of the children received a small toy, except Alice, who was only eight months old.

Christmas morning came, and the family had gathered for breakfast. Gus was seated at the end of the table, and the children were excited. "Pa, can we have some candy?" John asked eagerly.

"Not until you've finished breakfast."

Eva finished putting the meal on the table. Turning to John and Joe, she inspected their hands critically, "You boys had best wash your hands."

"Aw, Ma, we just washed 'em," they both protested.

"Well, do it again. They don't look clean to me."

John and Joe left the table reluctantly to comply with their mother's order. As they departed, Eva turned to Gus, "It's sure nice to have everybody home for a change."

About that time a cry from the bedroom interrupted them. Alice was awake and ready to be held. "I'll get her," Gus said, as he exited the room and disappeared down the hallway.

Finally, everybody was seated and the meal begun, after the blessing. John ate eagerly in anticipation of getting his candy, but Joe, who was usually a picky eater, simply pushed his food around on his plate.

"Joe, eat your breakfast," Gus prompted.

"I'm not very hungry," he replied.

"You can't have any candy until you eat your food."

"Aw, Pa."

"I mean it."

Hesitantly, Joe began to eat a spoonful of grits. He managed to get enough down to satisfy Gus.

John finished his food and pushed his plate back eagerly, "Pa, can I have some candy now?"

"I reckon. Just a little now, too much might make you sick."

Joe looked at Gus, but didn't say anything. "You can have some, too," Gus seconded.

Joe followed John to the living room where the tub of goodies were. Eva started to clear the table. Gus finished his cup of coffee and stood. "Here, Honey, let me help you," he said, as he picked up his plate and began to stack the dishes.

Gus and his family loaded their contributions to Christmas dinner in the back of "Leaping Lena" and went to Alonzo's. The family had gathered and were talking and laughing, as they prepared for the special meal.

Alonzo looked around and said, "Everybody's here, I think."

"Yeah, Gus's here. So everybody's here," Tom teased.

"Watch it, little brother, or I'll have to take you down a notch," Gus punched him lightly on the shoulder.

The family seated themselves for the meal. After Alonzo had said grace, they ate heartily. John was enjoying his second helping of dressing when he said to his grandmother, "Mammy, this is good."

"Why, thank you, John," she answered.

"This is just about the best Christmas we've ever had," John said, to no one in particular.

"Can't argue with that, John," Alonzo said, between bites on a chicken leg. "We're all together, and everybody's most well. My arthritis's acting up, but that ain't nothin' out of the ordinary."

Alonzo finished the drumstick and wiped his fingers on his napkin, "How long you gonna be home?" he asked Gus.

"Not long. We've got to start moving more rafts if we're gonna get all that timber to market before the river drops in the spring."

"It seems like you're always in a rush," Alonzo concluded.

Gus finished his cup of coffee, "Yeah, there never seems to be enough time to get everything done."

* * *

Gus was loading the wagon to go to the logging camp when John climbed on the seat and watched his father pack supplies in the wagon bed. "Pa?"

"What, son?"

"Can I go to the river with you sometime?"

"Oh, I reckon maybe later. What would you do on the river?"

"Same as you. I want to ride a raft all the way to the ocean. You've seen the ocean, ain't you, Pa? What's it like?"

"It's big. Monstrous big. You can look out over the water and not see land anywhere."

"What about the ships, Pa? Can you see ships on the ocean?"

"You sure can. You look way off out there and the first thing you see might be the top of a sail or a smoke stack, if she's a steamer."

"Did you ever ride on the ocean, Pa?"

"A few times, mostly between Darien and Brunswick."

"What's it like?"

"Well, it's pretty much like the river. We don't get out of sight of land really."

"Pa?"

"Yes?"

"When I get big like you, I'm gonna see the ocean. I'm gonna travel all over the world."

"Why, that's a right smart of travelin'. Here, how about you go ask your Ma to send me that basket of goodies she's been fixin' for me," Gus said, as he helped John down from the wagon seat.

John ran to the kitchen where Eva was finishing the basket of food. "Ma, Pa's ready for his basket."

"Okay, just hold your horses. I'll be right there."

Eva came out carrying the basket, holding John's hand. The other children followed. "Here you are. Do you have everything you need?"

"I think so," Gus answered, taking the basket and placing it under the wagon seat. "You young'uns take care of your Ma, now. I won't be gone too long. John, you mind your Ma and help her out with things. You're the man of the house while I'm away."

John stretched himself to his full height, proud to be singled out. "Yes, sir. I will."

Gus looked at Eva, then held out his arms to give her a hug. "I'll be home before you know it. Take care of yourself."

"I will. Be careful, Gus."

"Don't worry. I'll be extra careful."

Gus mounted the wagon and drove away. Eva and the children waved to him until he disappeared in the distance. "Okay, everybody, let's get our chores done. John, you feed the chickens."

"Aw, Ma. Do I hafta?"

"You heard what your Pa said."

"Yes'em."

* * *

The logging camp was as busy as a beehive when Gus arrived. There were two rafts waiting to be shipped. Gus stowed his gear and reported to the camp foreman.

"Gus, we've got to get this timber to market as soon as possible. There's a rumor that the price is about to drop, and we can't afford to take too much of a cut. With the labor we're payin', the cost is gonna eat us up if the price drops too low."

"We'll get it there. Give me two good men, and it'll be there in three days tops."

"Okay, take Ben and Lige, if that's all right with you?"

"That's fine. We'll leave within the hour."

The raft floated free of its moorings and headed down river. The day was young and Gus was sure he could make at least fifteen miles before sundown. There was a moon tonight, and he could run by moonlight, if necessary.

The weather didn't cooperate. An hour before nightfall, a cloud covered the sky, and it began to rain. There was no possibility of running at night in the rain. It was just too risky. Gus decided to tie the raft up for the night, or at least until the rain stopped.

A fire helped to fight the chill, but Ben's teeth were chattering from the cold. Gus looked at him and saw that he wasn't doing well. "Here, Boy, take this jacket and wrap yourself in it," Gus said, as he shed his leather coat and draped it over Ben's shoulders.

"Thanks," Ben said, between chattering teeth. "But what you gonna do, Gus? That's your jacket. Won't you get cold?"

"I'm fine, Boy. You just get yourself warm."

The rain ended, but the night remained back as pitch. No running tonight, Gus thought. We'll just have to make it up tomorrow.

Before the sun rose next morning, the raft was underway. The cloud cover remained, but began to break about noon. "Looks like we might make it after all," Gus said, to no one in particular. "The ole sun ball's startin' to come out."

Nightfall found them just above the narrows. This stretch of water was unlike any other on the river. Both banks were high bluffs with little or no access to the hill. Gus didn't fancy running the narrows at night, but thought he might chance it when the moon rose.

The raft lay moored to trees on the south side of the river as the raftsmen waited for moonrise. Gus lay down and pulled his hat over his face. "We'd best get some shut-eye. We've got a long night ahead of us, if Mr. Moon cooperates." He was asleep momentarily.

Gus awoke and looked around. The moon was rising over the tree tops in the east. "Time to rise and shine," he called, as he moved to the bow and prepared to cast off. The raft slid silently out of its berth and floated downstream between the high banks. "I'd hate to have to swim out of here and climb them walls," Gus said, as they moved quietly down river.

* * *

Captain Jack, who was in charge of the "Daisy Wheeler," had left Darien that afternoon and headed upriver with a cargo of freight. He and his skeleton crew had been indulging in the local tavern and were more suited to sleeping it off than piloting a steamboat on the river. To make matters worse, Captain Jack had bought two bottles for the trip. One for the crew, the other he held for himself. He took an occasional nip just to keep himself happy. By the time night had fallen, he was in no condition to command, much less steer the boat. He insisted that he was perfectly capable of handling things.

"Get the hell out of here and let me be," he said, with a thick tongue.

"Okay, you're the boss," his helmsman conceded.

Traffic was light, so there was little chance of a mishap, except that Jack almost grounded the boat once. Jack cussed himself, and everybody else on board for his drunken mistake, but insisted he was going to continue to steer.

There are those who insist that drunkenness is a victimless crime. They contend that the laws requiring drunks to be locked up for public intoxication are unfair. This thinking does not hold the individual responsible for his action. Many innocent persons have been seriously injured or lost their lives to just such people. Captain Jack was of the opinion that, as he put it, "It ain't nobody's damn business how much I drink and where I drink it."

The boat continued upstream. The crew seemed oblivious to the coming of night. By some miracle, Captain Jack managed to keep the steamer more or less in the channel. The moon rose over the larboard stern as they approached the lower end of the narrows. Captain Jack continued his joyride, paying no attention to the fact that he was now in a part of the river that required careful steering. A number of steamboats had sunk in the waters on this stretch of river.

* * *

Gus heard the sound of the steamboat long before it came in sight. He was prepared to steer right and give the steamer plenty of room to pass. "Okay, boys, pull'er to the hill as near as you can. We've got to make room for that smokestack comin' yonder."

His crew complied, and the raft was as close to the bank as they dared. They were now in a piece of water known as "Steamboat Cut." Gus remembered that at least one steamboat had sunk in this cut.

As the steamboat approached, the helmsman made no attempt to steer right. Gus saw what was happening, but there was little he could do. He began to wave his hat and shout at the steamboat. The boat kept coming. "Boys, we may have to ditch her!" he shouted, as the steamer showed no sign of veering.

Captain Jack could see something in the water ahead.

Vaguely, he thought he heard somebody shouting, but it was more like a dream than reality. He continued his course.

For just an instant, Gus thought they might make it. He stayed with the raft. After all, he didn't relish the thought of swimming in the icy water and he would lose control of the raft if he abandoned it. The steamboat kept coming.

The steamboat hit the raft on its left side, tearing it apart. The raft was well constructed, but it could never have withstood the impact of the steamboat. The force of the blow sent the raftsmen into the cold water. Logs spun crazily about them as the individual timbers did their own thing. Gus grabbed a log as it floated by and held on.

Looking around, he tried to spot his companions. "Ben! Lige!" He yelled. There was no answer.

Gus's boots felt as if they weighed a ton. He realized that there was no way he could swim with them on. He'd lost his hat as he hit the water. He had no choice, except to cling to the log until he could touch bottom and wade out of the river.

Gus could make out logs from the raft as they floated all around him, but there was no sight of his companions. After an eternity, Gus heard a voice. "Gus? Lige?"

"Over here," Gus called. "Is that you, Ben?"

"Yeah. God, this water's freezing!"

"Have you seen Lige?"

"Last I seen, he was trying to stay afloat on a log, but I ain't sure he made it."

Gus took a deep breath and swallowed hard. "Lige don't swim too good, if I remember right."

Gus looked up river. The steamboat was out of sight. If anybody had paid attention to the calamity they had caused, it wasn't obvious.

"Ben, we'll have to float down river to some place where we can wade out. These bluffs are almost impossible to climb, and I can't swim with these boots on. See if you can work yourself a little closer to me. We need to follow the main channel as close as possible. It would be better to climb the right bank. The left one would put us on the wrong side of the river."

Occasionally, one or the other of them would call Lige's name, but the result was always the same. The water seemed to get even colder, if that were possible. Gus thought he was losing the feeling in his feet. He was growing extremely tired, and began to wonder if he'd be able to maintain his grip on the log.

He kept shouting encouragement to Ben, "Hang in there, Boy, we're gonna make it out of this yet."

Ben didn't answer. He was saving his strength, but he was glad to have the sound of another voice so near. He renewed his grip on the log and hung on.

Gus considered trying to mount the log he was clinging to and pull off his boots. But he would probably lose them in the river and if that happened he would cut his feet in the swamp. He decided not to try it, not yet anyhow.

The moonlight shone on the river casting shadows from the trees high on the bluff. Once in awhile the shadows hid one or the other of the raftsmen.

Gus's body weighed a ton. He thought he'd never felt so heavy in his life. The cold water began to chill his chest and shoulders. Breathing became more difficult as circulation slowed due to the cold. He took frequent shallow breaths now in an attempt to keep his lungs filled with air.

The bluffs were not as high now. The river was broader here and the current wasn't quite so swift. Gus looked around to see if he could spot a sand bar or the mouth of a creek. Nothing met his eye.

Finally, he thought he could make out the mouth of a creek on the right of the river. "Ben, I think I see a possible landing. See if you can follow me. I'm gonna try and guide this splinter I'm ridin' into it."

Using the last of his reserve strength, Gus kicked a few strokes as he maneuvered the log toward the opening. The current from the creek caught him and pushed him downstream. Fortunately, an eddy caught the log and caused it to spin about and float upstream toward the creek. Gus extended his feet to try and find bottom. No such luck.

The log had made its closest approach to the bank and was beginning to float back into the downstream flow when Gus felt his feet touch bottom. Releasing the log, he stood in water up to his chin. He had to move. Ben's log had been caught by the eddy and was coming around for the first pass.

Gus stepped toward the bank and his head went under. Another step brought him above water again. He was now close enough to the bank to climb out without too much difficulty. Turning, he extended his hand and said, "Turn loose, Ben, and I'll help you up the bank."

Ben started to comply, then realized that he couldn't reach the extended hand. Gus stood still as the log made another circle in the eddy. This time the log hit the bank and Ben was able to stand on his feet. Both men climbed the bank, their feet slipping and their boots threatening to hold them down, as the mud sucked the boots like a giant sucking through a straw.

They fell on the leaves and Spanish moss and lay still exhausted from their ordeal. The water had been freezing, the air felt colder. Gus removed his boots and rubbed his feet. Slowly, he began to feel them again as the circulation returned.

"We're gonna need a fire," Gus said.

"How you gonna start a fire? You got a dry match on you, maybe?" Ben asked.

"Don't need matches if you know how to do it another way. Help me find something dry that'll burn."

Gus found a stump. Digging at the base, he uncovered a soft spot where the wood had begun to rot. Scraping out as much as he could, he placed it on some dry leaves. Using his pocket knife, he cut a small stick and sharpened the end to form a point. Placing the point in his pile of rotten wood, he began to rotate the stick between his hands. The friction caused the wood to smoke. Gus rested for a minute, and Ben worked the stick. Gus took another turn and, just as he was about to give it to Ben again, the smoldering became a spark and then a flame. Blowing on the flame carefully, Gus coaxed a higher fire. A supply of small twigs caught fire and soon the blaze warmed their hands. Finally, their bodies began to feel the warmth.

"Where'd you learn that trick?" Ben asked.

"From an Indian Chief I met one time."

Ben held his hands near the flames as he said, "Reckon where we are?"

"I'm not sure," Gus said. "But I figure we're at the mouth of Phenholloway Creek."

"How far's that from Jesup?"

"Not more'n fifteen or twenty miles, I'd guess."

"How're we gonna find our way out of here?"

"We'll just follow the creek, I reckon. There's probably folks living along it somewhere. The first thing we need, though, is some rest. Let's build up the fire and get some sleep."

Dawn came. The fire had died, but coals still smoldered underneath the ashes. Gus used a stick to stir the fire and added more fuel. Ben turned over and propped on his elbow. "What's for breakfast?" he asked.

"Steak and eggs," Gus replied.

"I wish."

"If this powder ain't wet in these cartridges, I'll see if I can shoot us some breakfast." Gus pulled his pistol from its holster.

Small game was plentiful in the river swamp. It was simply a matter of finding something that would supply their needs. Gus spied a squirrel scampering in a tree. Using both hands to steady his shot, he fired the weapon. The animal fell to a lower limb and seemed to hang on for an instant, then turned loose and hit the ground on a bed of leaves.

While Gus skinned and gutted the squirrel, Ben placed two forked sticks on each side of the fire and cut a stick for a spit. Some time later, the animal was skewered on the spit and roasted as fat dripped into the fire.

"How long before it'll be done?" Ben asked impatiently. "I'm starvin'."

"Won't be too long. I'm kind of hungry myself. That little swim we had last night sort of took the starch out of me."

Ben thought it must have been hours before Gus took the meat from the fire and cut a small strip with his knife. Tasting the cut, he nodded his head with satisfaction. "Here, try some," he handed the spit to Ben.

Ben cut a sample and tasted it. "Don't taste exactly like Ma's home cookin', but it ain't bad," he commented.

"Sorry about the seasonin'. But condiments are scarce as hen's teeth right this minute," Gus said, as he cut another strip of meat.

"No need to apologize. I'm so hungry I could eat horse meat."

Their meal complete, the men began their trek up the creek. A short distance upstream, they found an abandoned fishing boat. An inspection revealed why. The bottom had a hole the size of a man's fist near the stern. Gus looked at it and shook his head, "I don't know if we could patch her up or not. Guess we'll have to hoof it out of here."

"How about we put a piece of bark over the hole and try and seal it with tar?" Ben suggested.

"That might work. I don't fancy dragging through this swamp."

A cut of bark from a cypress knee supplied the patch. A search of the nearby pines supplied tar. The tar was spread generously around the hole on the underside of the boat and the bark patch applied over the tar. "If this works, it'll be a miracle," Gus said, as they finished pressing the bark in place.

"Here goes nothin'," Ben said, as they slipped the boat into the creek. The boat still leaked, but it wasn't too fast. They might just be able to pull it off.

Gus found a small sapling that had broken as a result of the fall of a larger tree. Placing it between the forks of a nearby oak, he broke it to a length that would serve as a boat pole.

The men boarded their makeshift craft and began to pole upstream. Occasionally, the water was too deep for the pole to reach bottom, so they had to drift back and come up along the bank. Ben would scoop water from the bottom of the boat with his hands while Gus poled their way upstream.

The sun was near its zenith when the two men spotted some sort of building ahead. Gus steered for the bank, and Ben jumped out and held the boat while Gus exited. Pulling the boat up on the bank, they turned toward the building.

A man and woman sat on the steps of the shack and watched them as they came up from the creek. "You fellers lost?" the man inquired, as they approached.

"You might say that," Gus answered. "Is there a road out of here? That floatin' coffin we've been travelin' in ain't the best transportation."

The man looked Gus and Ben over and decided they had been through a rough time from the looks of them. "What happened?" he asked curiously.

"Wreck. Steamboat hit us last night and tore our raft all to hell," Gus said.

"I'll be damned, you all right?"

"Near as I can tell. We need to get to the railroad."

The man showed more interest. "There's a trail out of here. Your best bet is to head for Gardi. You can catch a train there."

"How far?"

"Oh, I'd say seven to ten miles."

"Thanks."

"Say, you fellers had anything to eat?"

"Just a squirrel."

Turning to the woman, the man said, "Scare up some grub for these gents."

"Don't put yourself out none," Gus said.

"Ain't no trouble. Here, set a spell."

Gus and Ben enjoyed their new friend's hospitality and went on their way. Walking was more of a chore for Gus than he could remember. His chest felt sore and breathing was difficult.

Night fell as the raftsmen approached the settlement of Gardi. The train stopped here only if there were cars to be switched, but it could usually be flagged. The evening train from Brunswick should be along any time, they were told.

After what seemed hours, the sound of the train whistle was heard in the distance. The man in charge of the siding stepped onto the tracks and signaled with a red globed lantern. The train came to a stop. Gus and Ben thanked their benefactor and boarded the train.

Gus handed the conductor money for their fare and found a seat by the window. The train moved off slowly, picking up speed as the rhythm of the clicking rails increased. Gus would never have admitted it, but he was hurting. It was good to be going home. He could rest from his ordeal.

Chapter 16
The Sunset

The train rolled into Baxley about midnight. Gus and Ben, who were still exhausted from their ordeal on the river, still had to get home. There was no alternative to walking. Gus found it more and more difficult to exert himself. Frequent stops were needed as he and Ben made their way to the Reynolds farm. As they paused near Ten-Mile Creek, Gus found a log and seated himself. His breath was coming in short gasps as he struggled to fill his lungs with sufficient air.

"You all right?" Ben asked.

"I reckon. Just havin' trouble breathin'. That's all."

"You reckon you ought to see a doctor?"

"No, I don't think it'd do any good. I'm just tired. It seems like that exercise I got on the river has left me wore out. I just can't seem to get rested."

Gus coughed hard, but nothing came from his throat. He held his chest as the pain coursed through his body from the exertion. Ben felt helpless. He simply didn't know what to do. The fact was, he couldn't do anything that would make a real difference.

After a few minutes, Gus stood and steadied himself. He and Ben crossed the creek on the foot log and continued toward the farm. The moonlight cast shadows on the road and the breeze blowing through the trees made ghostly figures as it pushed the treetops. The sounds of the night were musical, but Gus was in no condition to appreciate them.

Another stop was necessary before they had finished the five or so miles from town to the farm. Gus recalled the time, not so long ago, when the five miles would have been a simple brisk exercise for him. Funny how a bit of time and circumstance could change things. His goal now was to get home and see his family and rest.

* * *

Eva heard footsteps on the porch and awakened from what had been a fitful sleep. The front door opened and voices came from the front room. Slipping out of bed, she found her robe and pulled it on. Tying her belt around her, she exited the bedroom. "Is that you, Gus?" she asked as she went into the living room.

"It's me, Honey," Gus answered. "Could you strike a light?"

Eva fumbled in the dark, found matches, lit the lamp, and adjusted the wick. Turning to Gus, she was astonished at his appearance. Instead of the usually hale and hearty man she was used to, there stood a haggard, pale, and breathless shadow of the former person.

"What in the world happened?" Eva managed to ask.

"We had an accident. A bad accident. Ben and me got out, but we lost our other man. We don't know what happened to him. Don't know if he's dead or alive."

Gus was short of breath from the brief speech. He sat down in a nearby chair and gasped for air. Eva was by his side instantly. She felt his forehead. He felt warm to her, but he was trembling as if he was cold.

She reacted immediately. "Here, give me your jacket, and I'll get you some warmer clothes. How about a warm drink?"

Gus pulled his jacket from his shoulders as Eva returned with a blanket to wrap around him. He lay back and tried to rest as she left the room for the kitchen.

Ben sat nearby watching, not knowing what he could or should do. He decided he'd stay, at least for awhile.

Eva lit a lamp in the kitchen and retrieved kindling from the wood box. It was the work of a few minutes to get a fire going. Placing the coffee pot on the stove, she prepared coffee to suit Gus's usual taste. Then she returned to the front room to check on Gus.

He seemed to be breathing easier now. In fact, he was so quiet she thought he might be asleep. She touched his forehead again. There was little or no change in his fever. Gus stirred.

"Honey, why don't you get undressed and go to bed? I'll bring your coffee when it's ready."

"That's not necessary. I'll be all right here for now."

Ben stood and spoke, "Mrs. Reynolds, is there anything I can do? Maybe fetch a doctor?"

"I don't know. The best thing to do now is get him in bed and get something warm in him. We'll send for the doctor if that don't help."

"Well, ma'am, I just wanted to help if I could."

"I appreciate it, but I think you might need to rest as much as Gus. How're you feelin'?"

"I'm tired ma'am, but I don't feel sick."

"That's good. Why don't I get you a blanket and you can bed down for the night? I don't have an extra bed, but you're welcome to sleep here in the livin' room."

"Thank you kindly, ma'am."

Eva brought the coffee for Gus and an extra cup for Ben. She handed Ben a cup and turned to give Gus a hand with his. Gus reached for the cup. His hand trembled as he attempted to hold it. Coffee sloshed over the brim of the cup as his hand shook.

"Here, let me help you," Eva offered.

She held the cup while Gus took a short sip. He lay back for a moment, and then indicated he was ready for another drink. Eva helped him finish the cup.

She stood and said, "Come on, I'll help you to our bed."

Gus rose shakily and leaned on her arm as they made their way to the bedroom. Eva helped him undress and get into bed, then she wrapped him in bed clothes. After a time, the trembling ceased, and he drifted off into a fitful sleep. Eva spent the rest of the night sitting by their bed watching as Gus tossed and turned occasionally in his sleep.

Dawn came quietly. Gus lay in bed where he had slept restlessly for the past few hours. The morning sun shone through the curtains, casting a bright light on the bed covers. Gus opened his eyes and looked around. Eva had dozed off in a chair near the bed. Outside, the wind howled around the corner of the house making a mournful sound.

Gus stirred slightly and coughed. Eva was awake instantly. "How do you feel?" she asked.

Gus coughed again and managed to catch his breath. "Like I'm burnin' up."

She was by his side, feeling his forehead. The heat seemed to burn her hand. Leaving the room, she soon returned with a basin of water and a towel. Wetting the towel, she laid it on his brow as he lay back in the covers. Gus lay still and took deep breaths. Another cough racked his whole body as he clutched his chest.

"Where do you hurt?" Eva asked.

"My chest. It feels like I can't hardly breathe, and when I cough my whole chest hurts something awful."

Eva left the room and returned with a jar. "Here, let me rub some of this on you."

Gus allowed her to pull the bedclothes down and open his undershirt. She applied the salve generously to his chest. It was cold and almost sent him into another chill, but finally it began to turn warm and soothe his chest. Wrapping him in the bedclothes again, Eva placed the salve on the dresser and wiped her hand on a cloth.

"Thanks, that feels better," Gus managed a weak grin.

A knock at the door drew Eva's attention. It was Ben. "Pardon me, ma'am, but I was wonderin' how Gus was ?"

Eva went to the door and pulled it shut behind her. "He's still in a bad way. I was wonderin' if you'd go tell his Ma and Pa about him bein' sick?"

"Sure will. Is there anything else I can do?"

"I reckon not. Say, you ain't had a bite of breakfast. Tell you what, you go see if his Ma can come, and I'll make us some breakfast."

"Ma'am, you don't have to do that. I can see you ain't hardly slept a wink. It's too much trouble."

"It ain't no trouble a'tall. My young'uns will be up soon hungry as bear cubs. Now go along."

Susie and Alonzo were there in short order. Susie took charge of fixing the breakfast while Eva sat beside Gus and kept an eye on him. He dozed and came in and out of sleep for the next hour.

After awhile, Susie came into the room carryin' a breakfast plate for Eva. "Here, you need to eat something," she urged.

"Thank you," Eva said, as she tasted the food.

There was nothing wrong with the food, but she set it aside.

"Eat, child. You've got to keep up your strength," Susie admonished her.

"I'm sorry, Ma, I ain't very hungry. I'll go fix Gus some soup."

"No, you won't. I'll fix it. Why don't you lay down for awhile? You ain't slept all night."

"I'll rest awhile after I give Gus something."

Susie returned presently with a bowl of hot steaming soup. She seated herself near the bed. She looked at Eva. She was about to fall from her chair as weariness overtook her body. Susie set the soup on the table by the bed and went to Eva. Placing her arm around Eva, she helped her to a bed in the next room.

* * *

Eva slept the sleep of exhaustion. The sun was high in the sky when she awoke. She was startled as she sat up, trying to remember what had happened. In the back of her mind, she thought she remembered Gus was home, but it was more like a bad dream than reality.

She found her way into the bedroom where Gus lay. Susie was sitting beside him reading her Bible, her lips moving silently as she looked at the words on the page. It wasn't a dream after all. Gus lay just as she remembered. He seemed to be resting. That was good. The rest would make all the difference.

Susie looked up. "How're you feelin', daughter?" she asked as she laid aside the book.

"I'm okay. How's Gus?"

"He's had a rough day, but he's restin' now. You had anything to eat?"

"No. I came straight here to check on Gus."

"Why don't you let me fix you something? You can sit with Gus while I get it ready."

Susie left the room and went to the kitchen. Eva felt Gus's brow. She thought he still had a fever, but perhaps it wasn't as high as it had been. She sat and held his hand as she prayed silently.

Susie came through the door with a plate of food. "This'll help you get your strength back," she offered, as she handed the plate to Eva.

Eva took the plate and said in a startled voice, "Oh, my God! Where's that boy that Gus had with him? What's his name? Ben?"

Susie looked toward the door, "He's still out there settin' with Alonzo, I think. Why?"

"I'd completely forgot about him. Is he okay?"

"As far as I know. We told him he could go on home, but he said he weren't in no hurry. Said Gus saved his life on the river, and he weren't gonna leave him just yet."

Gus had a restless night. Eva and Susie took turns sitting with him. Cold compresses on his forehead helped cool the fever and frequent rubs with the salve helped ease his chest pain.

On the morning of the second day, he had not improved a great deal. Alonzo was of the opinion that they should send for the doctor, since their home remedies didn't seem to be working. Eva had mixed feelings. She wanted the best for Gus, but she still hesitated to put him in the hands of a doctor. On the third day, when it seemed there was no change for the better, she consented.

Ben, who had insisted on staying until Gus was better, volunteered to go for the doctor. Eva told him how to find Dr. Bratcher, and he returned with the doctor in a couple of hours.

"Let me have a look at him," Dr. Bratcher said, as he leaned over the bed. He checked Gus's pulse, felt his neck for swollen glands, and listened to his heart and lungs. "Help me turn him over," he directed. An examination of his back completed, the doctor stood up and looked at Eva.

"Mrs. Reynolds, I'd say he has a real bad respiratory infection. At least a severe chest cold, maybe worse. There may be fluid in the lungs. Has he coughed up any thing?"

Eva thought for a second, "Not that I recall. He's had a hard, dry cough ever since he got home, but I don't think he spit up anything much."

"That sounds good, but we need to keep an eye on it. If he starts to cough up anything at all, let me know."

* * *

In her distress over Gus's illness, Eva had almost forgotten her children. They hadn't been abandoned. Susie had taken them under her wing and carried them to her home. Their aunts helped look after them, but they were concerned for their father and needed to be reassured. While Susie sat with Gus, Eva made her way to the big house to spend a few minutes with them.

John, who was usually the most vocal, asked his mother, "Ma, is Pa okay?"

Eva smiled at John as she shifted Alice to get a better hold on her. "Your Pa's real sick, young'uns. We don't know just how bad it is. I want you to stay here with Mammy and Pappy until he's better. Promise me you'll mind and help when you're needed."

"We promise, Ma," they answered in unison.

Joe, who had been standing on one foot most of the time, shifted and looked at Eva, "Ma, is Pa gonna die?"

"What makes you ask?"

"My kitty got sick, and he died."

"Honey, everybody that gets sick don't die."

"Yes'em. I just wondered."

"We're gonna do all we can to get your Pa well. It's gonna take some time though. You can help by being real good. Now go wash up for supper."

* * *

On the afternoon of the fifth day, Gus awoke and Eva was seated by his side. "What time is it?" he asked faintly.

Eva leaned over so that she could hear him better, "It's near five o'clock in the evenin'. Why?"

Gus struggled to sit up. Eva caught him and placed a pillow under his shoulders. Gus looked out the window. The evening shadows were long, and the sun glistened on the treetops out his bedroom window. He looked at Eva. "I want to see the sunset," he whispered.

"What did you say, honey?"

"I want to breathe some fresh air and see the sunset."

Eva found Susie in the kitchen and told her what Gus wanted. Susie agreed to help her. Together they steadied Gus between them and placed him in a rocking chair they had covered with a blanket. Covering him against the afternoon chill and placing a stool under his feet, they sat with him as the day drew to a close.

The sun had begun to hide behind the treetops in the west. Its rays shone through the pines and cast a swaying shadow over the chair where Gus was seated. He gazed at the sun as it made its way into its night cave. He thought it must have been the most beautiful sunset he had ever witnessed. Night fell and the evening star shown red in the dusk. Gus had no way of knowing it, but this was the planet Mars, named for the Roman god of war. It was at least symbolic of the battle he had fought all his life, and continued to fight. The battle to survive.

"Hadn't we better get you back inside?" Eva asked.

Gus looked at her. "Okay."

As Eva and Susie lifted him to move him inside a fit of coughing racked his body and he began to spit up. Eva looked at it, realizing her worst fears. The spittle was a brownish color.

* * *

Dr. Bratcher came as soon as he was notified. He did the routine check and then laid aside his instruments. He didn't say anything right away. Nodding to Eva, he walked to the next room. She followed, dreading what he might say. Curiously, people hesitate to talk around the sick because they might overhear what is said and somehow be ill affected by it.

"What's wrong?" Eva asked.

"I don't know how to tell you this," Dr. Bratcher said, hesitantly. He had never gotten used to giving families bad news in all his years of practice. "But Gus has pneumonia."

"Pneumonia? How bad is it?" Eva asked, afraid to hear the answer.

"It's bad. Really bad. I've never seen a worse case."

"What are his chances of gettin' better?"

"Slim to none, I'm afraid."

Eva put her hands over her face and sobbed silently into them. After a moment, she composed herself and faced Dr. Bratcher. "How long does he have?"

"It's hard to say. A week. Maybe ten days."

"What can I do?"

"Just keep him comfortable, mostly. Just what you've been doing. I'll check back with you each day. Send for me if he gets worse."

Eva seldom left Gus's side. She ate, slept, and watched over him in the same room day and night. His pain grew progressively worse. His breathing became shallower and shallower. At times, it seemed he would breathe his last, but somehow he recovered and continued to breathe.

On the eleventh day, he didn't spit up at all. Eva noticed that he was having even more trouble breathing. The lapses between breaths were longer and longer. She sent for the doctor once again.

Dr. Bratcher came and examined Gus. He shook his head and walked from the room. It was just a matter of time.

Gus lingered through the night. Dr. Bratcher stood by his bedside amazed at the struggle, as he persisted. The sun broke through the trees, giving light to the world. Gus struggled for breath. One gasp followed another. Dr. Bratcher stood beside him holding his wrist. The pulse stopped as Gus failed to catch his breath on the last gasp. His soul departed his body at his favorite time of day. Gus had always thought of each day as a fresh new beginning. The world was refreshed and new, and so was he.

Eva had been by his side until the end. She looked at the doctor and said, "He's gone, isn't he?"

"I'm afraid so."

* * *

Eva felt one burden descend on the other she already carried. She had never considered the fact that she might have to bury Gus someday. Where could she put him? There were family cemeteries near their home, but with Gus gone this might not be their home for long. After some soul searching, she decided to bury him in the soil she loved best. Her childhood home had a beautiful place in the woods with sandy soil and trees all around. Gus would have liked that.

Susie would have preferred to bury Gus near her home so that his grave could have been tended, but this wasn't her decision. After all, Eva was his wife, and she had the final say in the matter.

Eva had very little money. What with the doctor bills and other expenses, she would barely get by. Gus had been a good provider, but like so many of us, he had not made provision for his family against his death. A pine casket was as good as she could afford.

Gus's body was washed carefully and dressed in his best suit. Friends and neighbors brought food and helped with the preparation of the body. The neighbors remained through the night and comforted Eva as best they could. The funeral had been planned for the next day.

When all was ready, the casket was placed in the two-horse wagon, and the long journey to the Hester's home began. They took the same trail through the woods that Gus had traveled so many times. The familiar trees cast their shadows on the coffin as the horses pulled their burden through the wild and beautiful forest. The streams washed the axles of the wagon as it bore its burden along the trail. The call of the forest creatures, from the bark of a squirrel to the chirp of a katydid, punctuated the silence with a music that Gus would have loved.

Eva and the children rode in a buggy behind the wagon carrying the coffin. All were quiet. The sound of the horses hooves made a rhythmic clatter on the earth. The pace was slow, but Eva was in no hurry. As far as she was concerned, Gus could be buried later than sooner.

Other members of the Reynolds' family followed along in the funeral train. Slowly, the procession made its way along the dirt road. More than half a day later, they arrived at the Hester's home.

Bill and Annie were there to meet them, along with Eva's brothers and sisters. The wagons paused while the mourners dismounted and refreshed themselves in the Hester's home. Word had reached friends and family of the tragic loss that Eva had suffered, and they had responded generously by bringing food and drink to the house for the family and others who were attending the funeral.

Eva saw that the children were fed. She ate nothing herself. She was too full of grief and too nervous to keep food on her stomach.

The grave diggers came to the house and quietly reported that the grave was ready. The family began to prepare to leave for the grave site. The coffin, which had been opened temporarily for viewing the body, was nailed shut for the last time and placed in the wagon bed. The procession moved slowly around the corner of the field with most of the mourners walking behind the buggy carrying Eva and her family. Nobody talked. The jingle of harness chains and an occasional snort from a horse were the only sounds.

The wagon stopped near the grave and the pallbearers lifted the casket from the wagon and placed it on two boards laid across the grave. Two ropes hung underneath the casket. These would be used to lower the coffin into the grave.

The family gathered around the grave and stood quietly while their friends gathered behind them. The minister stood on the west end of the grave. His shadow fell on the coffin as he opened his

Bible and began to speak.

"Friends, we are gathered here to commit the earthly body of our friend and loved one to the earth. God said to Adam, 'Dust thou art and to dust thou shalt return.' But Jesus said, 'Whosoever believeth in me, though he were dead, yet shall he live.' So, we have hope even in this dark hour, that we will live again....'"

Eva didn't hear much more of the minister's remarks. Her heart felt as if it would tear itself from her bosom, and her mind wandered through memories of her life with Gus. Once more, in memory, they walked down a moonlit lane together. They shared a dance and held each other in a gentle and loving embrace. Gus smiled at her and teased her about some small thing. He gave her some trinket to wear, or gave her a Christmas present that she'd have never guessed he would've thought about. He held her hand as their babies were born, and he gathered her in his arms after a long absence and whispered sweet things in her ear.

There was no way to measure the length of the funeral service in Eva's mind. It might have been five minutes or five hours. There was simply no passing of time in her mind.

"Amen," the minister said.

The pallbears moved to the grave and caught the ropes, lifting the coffin high enough to remove the boards. As a voice sang *Amazing Grace*, the casket was lowered into the grave. Shovels of earth made a hollow sound on top of the coffin as the grave was filled with dirt.

Eva and the children mounted the buggy and made their way toward the house. The mourners began to drift away. Some of them went back to the house, but others stayed until the grave was filled.

The grave diggers finished filling the grave and mounded the extra soil on the top. Shovels were used to pack the earth, and tree limbs were placed over it to discourage animals from digging in the fresh grave. The grave diggers finished their work and picked up their tools. Those who were standing nearby took one last look at the grave and made their way to the house.

The sun sank in the west and dusk began to fall. Far off in the woods, a whipoorwill called. The Planet Mars, the warrior god, appeared in the western sky, as it had for perhaps millions of years. The night creatures began their songs, and the air was filled with music from their calls. Although he couldn't hear them, Gus's body was surrounded by the sounds he loved.

Meanwhile, back at the house, Eva had taken care of the children, and they were sitting with their grandparents. She made her way to her old bedroom. It hadn't changed in ten years. She looked around at the furniture and felt right at home. Sitting on the edge of what was once her bed, she stared off into space and tried to erase the flood of pain and thoughts coursing through her mind and body.

She lay back across the bed and breathed a silent prayer. What about tomorrow? Gus was gone. How could she face the future without him? Turning on her stomach, she poured out her grief in a torrent of tears. She poured out her soul in anguished prayer. After some time, she was able to think more clearly. She remembered somewhere that someone had said, "Time heals all wounds." Yes, that was what she needed, time. But even as she contemplated it, another thought crossed her agonized mind. Time might ease the pain, but the love would never die.

Epilogue

Gus was gone, or was he? True, his body lies buried in a grave, but his memory lives. It lives in the hearts of his children, grandchildren, and great-grandchildren. It lived for fifty plus years in the heart of Eva, the one who, perhaps, loved him more than any mortal could comprehend.

His spirit inspired his descendants to do things that even he would not have believed. His spirit inspired those who were his friends and caused them to pass on the legacy that made others what they were to some extent. Some say that his ghost walks the hills of Jeff Davis County to this day. Not in a malicious manner, but with kindness. George Hester claimed to have seen him on a number of occasions. Eva had dreams or visions of him as long as she lived.

His pioneer spirit lives in the heart and mind of his descendants. From the grave, he inspires them to reach out to new frontiers. He loved the natural beauty of this earth and would have fought to preserve it.

You won't find him in the history books. As far as historians are concerned, he might never have lived. He was a simple man who did not crave the limelight, so his name is missing, even from the chronicles of his home county.

Can such a man truly be gone? I think not. As long as your memory lives and your influence is felt, there is no doubt in my mind that you exist.

For additional copies of *River Pilot*, or other titles, please contact:

Double Eagle Enterprises, Inc.
735 Liberty Circle
Murphy, NC 28906
Phone:828-494-BOOK